I0822310

Attack From Within

James Bultema

P.D. Publishing
Scottsdale, AZ

ALSO BY JAMES BULTEMA

Fiction
Sea of Red

Non-Fiction
Guardians of Angels: A History of the Los Angeles Police Department 1869 – 2019

Unsolved Cold-Case Homicides of Law Enforcement Officers

The Protectors: A Photographic History of Police Departments in the United States

Gangsters and Cops: Prohibition, Corruption, and LAPD's Scandalous Coming of Age

Documentary
Behind the Badge: An Insiders History of the Los Angeles Police Department

P.D. Publishing

First Edition

Website: https://www.jamesbultema.com

This book was edited by Jennifer Duty
Cover design by Momir Borocki
Author photo by Carole Bultema

ISBN 979-8-9880751-9-6 Paperback
ISBN 979-8-9880751-3-4 Hardback
ISBN 979-8-9880751-4-1 Ebook

Chapter 1

Ali Al Salem Air Base

Kuwait

"Hurry, Tim, I want a shot before those pricks reach the city."

"Come on, Frank, you need to close the distance to the HVT if you want confirmation."

"What do you think I'm doing, Tim." As he argued with his enlisted sensor operator, Frank, piloting the RPA, Remotely Piloted Aircraft, accelerated from his cruising speed of 150 knots, pushing his 950-horsepower MQ-9 Reaper drone quickly to 260 knots. "Closing on target," he said calmly, forcing his heart to stop beating so hard.

"Gentlemen," chimed in the Mission Intelligence Coordinator, Major Jennie Armstrong, "keep it together; we can't mess this up."

Captain Frank Rodgers had every right to be jittery. For a job that is 99 percent monotonous, he was basking in the one percent pure adrenaline rush this mission provided. This is precisely why he signed on the dotted line six years ago and joined the United States Air Force.

"We are three miles out," said sensor operator Tech Sergeant Tim Withers, "the truck is heading west on Highway 36; we should have confirmation shortly."

"Good job, Tim." Looking up at his sizeable high-resolution monitor, Tim saw the dust trail from his target but not well enough to confirm this was his man. His Reaper was closing the distance quickly.

Throwing up dust on Highway 36 in their 2002 Toyota pickup truck were Islamic Revolutionary Guard Major General Foroohar Nakhjevani and Kourosh Ormazd, a high-ranking member of Hezbollah. The two terrorists had recently been identified as the brain trust behind 2020 Operation Martyr Soleimani, the most significant ballistic missile attack ever against Americans, injuring 110 troops stationed at al-Asad Airbase in Iraq. With orders from the president of the United States, Mark Taylor, it was time for payback. And fulfilling those orders were Rodgers and Withers, who were targeting the men behind it all.

"I have eyes on the HVT," Frank blurted out, cutting through the silence. "Verifying this is the correct target?"

"You got it, Frank, I concur. The truck has the correct license plate, color, and year and carries two male occupants."

"I agree," stated Major Armstrong, who oversaw the operation and sat in the same metal command center as her crew. "Permission to launch weapons."

Going through his checklist, Frank was confident with his targeting information. He sent an electronic signal to the two AGM-114 air-to-ground Hellfire missiles strapped snugly under the wings of the Reaper. He calmly pulled the trigger on his joystick. "Missiles away," he said as the rockets released from the MQ-9, the missiles shot towards the two unsuspecting, most-wanted extremists in the world. Guided by Frank, the laser from the drone kept the target in its sights. With the combined speed of the missiles' motors and gravity, by the time the warheads reached their target they were traveling at the speed of sound, giving the terrorists no time to evade.

Within seconds, the monitors in the room flashed bright red and orange as two hundred pounds of high explosive energy obliterated what was once a Toyota truck. When the dust settled, there was no truck, and two of the most wanted terrorists in the world were no more. High fives went up around the room.

Chapter 2

Muslim Center of Michigan

Dearborn, Michigan

One thing about stakeouts is that they are tedious as hell. FBI Special Agent Harley Jennings knew this firsthand. He and his partner, Ali Mohsen, were on their fifth hour of babysitting a known gangbanger from the Warren Bros—a Muslim street gang. They operated around the agents' turf in Dearborn, just outside Detroit, Michigan. The two men were out of the FBI's Counterterrorism Division (CTD), specifically ITOS-II, the International Terrorism Operations Section specializing in non-al Qaeda groups such as Hezbollah. They were working a lead that the suspect was having thoughts of making a connection with a known member of Hezbollah.

The agents had nicknamed him LM, as in lead man, or simply asshole. They weren't picky.

"Do you believe the balls on this guy?" asked Ali. "He's heading straight to the Muslim Center."

"Hell," said Harley, "no one ever accused these pricks of being smart."

"I know, but the mosque?"

As LM walked by the American flag swirling in the wind in front of one of the largest mosques in North America, the agents noticed an older middle eastern man coming from the mosque, walking down the long path and stopping to greet LM. Harley quickly took some pictures. Then, just as fast, the two men returned to the massive religious shrine and were lost to sight as the large front door closed behind them.

"Now what?" asked Ali. "Should I go in and see what's going on?"

"I think so," said Harley. "Put your comms on and act just like any other Muslim going to pray."

"Got it. I'll stay in touch." With that, Ali was out the door and walking down the same path to the mosque as the men he was tailing. Along the way, he ensured his Glock 19M stayed hidden from view.

Ali had a history. In April 1983, a suicide bombing of the United States embassy in Beirut, Lebanon, killed sixty-three people: thirty-two Lebanese, seventeen Americans, and fourteen other visitors. Tragically, Ali's father, who was employed at the embassy, was among those who perished. Ali's mother, pregnant with Ali at the time, made the difficult decision to relocate to Dearborn shortly after Ali's birth. There, she sought solace and support from relatives while raising her only child.

As a Muslim born in Lebanon, Ali fit in seamlessly with the 190,000 Arab Americans living in Metro Detroit, including their neighbors in Dearborn, many of whom were of Lebanese descent.

Ali grew up in a home full of love and learned to speak Arabic from those around him. He attended the University of Michigan. During his senior year, Ali's class from the Global Security and Intelligence Studies program was invited by the FBI's Deputy Assistant Director to visit Washington, DC. This experience and conversations with other Bureau members convinced Ali that he wanted to pursue a career in counterterrorism. The desire to confront the terrorist who took his father's life further motivated him.

As Harley watched, Ali speed-walked to the entrance. Over comms, he could hear Ali’s breathing pick up as he disappeared into the massive structure. The retired combat Marine could barely take not being by his partner's side, but he knew he would stand out like a wolf in a sheep's pen.

Ali entered the vast circular prayer room and saw it was empty. He quickly stopped, forcing his breathing to slow down so he could listen for any telltale sound of the two men. Nothing.

The building was too large to go room to room, so he acted on his hunch and headed down the hall to the library. "Harley, there's no sign of them heading to the library."

"Roger that," came the reply.

As soon as Ali entered the library, he was greeted by an enormous man who looked nothing like a librarian. Instead, he looked like someone who would just as soon break you in half as guide you to the reference section. Even his long, straggly beard seemed oversized. The dude must be over six-six and three hundred pounds, thought Ali. As he looked up to make eye contact with the giant, the man whispered, "May I help you?" in a voice better suited for someone half his size.

Thinking quickly, Ali said calmly, "Yes, I'm new in the community and was anxious to scan your books to see what might interest me."

"Why yes, how delightful," said the giant. "But unfortunately, the librarian had to step out and won't return today. She asked me to lock up the library for her."

"That's okay; I'll just be a minute." With that, Ali moved towards the racks, but a gigantic hand reached out and firmly stopped him in his tracks.

"I'm so sorry," said the giant, "but I have strict instructions to close the library—now." With "now," the giant let his voice control slip, and it came out in the deep, gruff voice of a man who is used to giving orders—and having them obeyed.

Looking at the eyes perched way above his five-foot-eight frame, Ali decided not to push it. "Sure, I understand. I'll come back another day." With that, he slowly turned towards the exit, but as he did so, he caught a reflection in a side window of the two men several aisles down, between the racks. He casually said, "Thanks again," and headed for the main entrance.

Walking towards the front, he contacted Harley, "Did you hear that? I saw our two men; they were hiding in the back of the library. I'll be right there and fill you in."

"Sounds good. I have relocated to Pizza Place on Brace Street by the freeway. Meet me there. I don't want to blow our cover."

Sitting in a corner booth with eyes on the front door, the two FBI agents debriefed. "I definitely think we have something here," said Ali. They do a meet and greet out front for whatever reasons but immediately beat feet to the library. Throw in this giant asshole to ensure no one interferes, and you have my suspicions raised. This was not a church visit."

Harley sipped his Coke and said, "Yeah, I agree. This gangbanger isn't there to cleanse his soul; he's up to something. It can't be good when a gang member meets with a possible Hezbollah terrorist. My hunch is they are teaming up, and I wouldn't say I like it. I'll write it up, shoot it upstairs, and try to get us more resources. Hopefully, some of the photos I took will come back with an ID.

Sound good?"

"Yeah, I agree." Both silently wondered what they had turned up.

Chapter 3

Bekaa Valley, Lebanon

Revolutionary Training Camp 5

Ahmad Nadar was no ordinary Hezbollah terrorist newbie. The twenty-two-year-old was American and got off to a dismal start when he showed up in Beirut unannounced, armed with a pistol, demanding to join the forces fighting the infidels. "Not so fast," he was told. The Lebanese were very skeptical of the American, no matter how much he chattered of his devotion to Allah. But if sincere, he would be an excellent asset for Hezbollah.

From the beginning, Nadar stood out as a brilliant person. Hezbollah was interested. After an intensive background check, the interrogators knew his history as well as his mother did.

Ahmad was raised in Mississippi, the only child of an American mother and a Lebanese father. Growing up, Ahmad stood out due to his distinctive features, reflecting his Lebanese heritage. At five foot nine but of stocky build with a head of thick black hair, brown eyes, and a dark olive complexion, the young man looked nothing like all the natural-born American kids. Being different, he was bullied endlessly.

Growing up following 9/11, with a nation's seeming hatred for almost anyone who looked like America's newest enemy, Ahmad was regularly beaten by the white kids in school. At first, he didn't fight back because of his Muslim faith and being a man of peace. This detached attitude further enraged his enemies.

The ringleader of this hate group was Bobby Brown, an overweight kid with a huge belly, who was strong enough to bench-press his gym teacher. Bobby earned the respect of the other kids in school because he thumped anyone who dared pester him for being fat.

Because of punks like Bobby, Ahmad went to his father, asking if Allah would not forsake him for learning to fight back. His father said that Allah proclaims using jihad to defend one's faith and oneself is necessary in certain circumstances. He told his son this was one of them. Over time, Ahmad learned to fight, mainly how to box, but hid his ability until he felt confident he could win.

That day came soon enough when Bobby, with three of his dirtbag friends, stopped Ahmad as he walked home from school. Bobby got in Ahmad's face while the other three punks surrounded him. "Hey, you fucking raghead, you haven't paid me your lunch money for two weeks. So, I'm not asking now, but instead have decided it's time to kick your ass again, you little fuck."

With that, one of the boys jumped on Ahmad's back, knocking him to the ground. Immediately, they all started kicking him. But this time, the young Muslim was prepared. In boxing, he had learned to cover up, protecting himself until he could gain the advantage. Unexpectedly, Ahmad jumped up yelling as loud as he ever had in his life, "Make your peace, for Allah has blessed me to kick your butts." Swiftly, Ahmad jumped up and went straight for Bobby, using his momentum to land a powerful right to his nose, shattering it and spraying blood over everyone. The other three kids froze as if saying, "What the hell," giving Ahmad time to land another right to the kid standing nearest him, knocking him out with one punch. He fell to the ground as if being folded like a Persian rug. Ahmad quickly got in his boxing stance, ready to strike the other two, who took one look at this fighting monster they never knew existed and took off running as fast as they could back towards the school.

Ahmad bent over the sobbing Bobby, who was choking on his blood. He grabbed his shirt, lifting his head from the ground. Getting inches from his face, Ahmad said, "Listen, you fat prick, if you or any of your punk-ass friends bother me again, I will come after you, and no matter where we are, I will kill you." With that, Ahmad threw him back to the ground and gave him a final kick to the ribs. He casually picked up his books, and slowly turned towards home, a changed man.

Back at school the next day, Ahmad felt like a new person and dressed just how he felt. Since the American kids never accepted him as one of them anyway, Ahmad went in the other direction. He made it a point to dress in traditional Lebanese clothes like his father. He adorned himself with multi-layered baggy trousers known as sherwals, a white shirt, vest, jacket, and an outlandish headdress wrapped around his head and settled on his shoulders. News swiftly circulated throughout the school about the Lebanese kid who kicked Bobby Brown's ass and broke his nose with a single punch.

It wasn't long before Ahmad garnered a group of devoted followers who, like him, had experienced bullying and now regarded him as their fearless leader. The white kids gave them a wide berth in the hallways and around town.

Over the next few years, Ahmad immersed himself in the preachings of Allah and the videos produced by Hezbollah, campaigning for the destruction of Israel and expelling Americans from the Middle East. He felt a calling that he must do his part. He decided to forsake the US. He traveled to Lebanon to become a terrorist to bring about the reappearance of the Iman—the Shite Islamic Messiah.

The young man quickly distinguished himself among his peers at the training camp in the expansive hills of the Bekaa Valley, thanks to his sharp intellect and unwavering devotion to his religion. In the classroom, conducted in metal sheds hidden among the mountains, usually under large trees, he learned to read maps and apply them to ambush skills taught by his Lebanese superiors and an Iranian from the Islamic Revolutionary Guard Corps, IRGC. Ahmad soon became an expert with his AK-47, preferring it to the American-made M16. Moving on to machine guns, he was an excellent marksman using the Russian-made PK.

After completing his forty-five-day combat course, Colonel Masoud Shahryar, the lead Iranian instructor from IRGC, approached Ahmad.

"Tell me, Nadar, why do you choose to fight with Hezbollah against the people that oppress us, including your own country?"

Ahmad paused, his gaze locked with the colonels before responding. "Colonel, I don't think of myself as an

American but as a Muslim with my belief in Allah. All my life, I have been persecuted for my ideologies, how I look and dress, and even how I act. No, I don't feel a bond with the US—this is my country now and the one I swear allegiance to."

Ahmad took a breath as the colonel nodded for him to continue. "Believe me, I fully understand and concur with the objective of Hezbollah to eliminate the entire state of Israel and every Jew who lives there. But from my perspective, there is no difference between the US and Israel. The Americans work in complete accord with Israel. I want to be a fighting soldier to bring the Holy War to the country I no longer call home. Allah has blessed me to lead men in battle, which is why I'm here."

"Nadar," said the colonel, "those are strong words, but I and others believe we are all sons of the ummah, the part of Allah, the vanguard of which was made victorious by God in Iran. You have proven yourself these past six weeks, and the faqih has faith in you as you take your next step as a fighter for our Muslim faith. Now prepare yourself for a trip to my country of Iran. Praise Allah.

Chapter 4

Tip a Few

Dearborn, Michigan

LM, whose real name was Umair Sabar, sat where he always did, in the rear corner booth with eyes on the rest of the patrons. Tip a Few was a local bar catering to young Muslims, who were not devout and liked to drink mostly beer, including most of his gang—Warren Bros. Tip a Few was a dive, plain and simple. It had plaster constantly falling from the ceiling and paint flaking from the walls. But Umair put up with it for one reason: the owner had the best shamshir sword collection he had ever seen. The sight of so many alluring curved blades decorating the otherwise dreary wall behind the bar made him reflect on his heritage. He was a proud Lebanese man.

During moments of solitude, Umair would let his imagination run wild. He would envision his ancestors mounted on powerful horses, skillfully wielding their shamshir swords as they bravely fought off hordes of enemy warriors, repelling the endless invasions of his homeland.

Umair's homeland was Lebanon, but his life took a significant turn. One day his mother relocated them to

Dearborn after his father mysteriously disappeared and never returned home. Where he went, Umair didn't know and didn't care. His mom seemed not to care either, as she went through men like so much candy in a jar. Some of these men would spend a few nights laying around the house, ordering then eleven-year-old Umair around to ensure they were never out of beer. If he were slow to respond, several of the jerks would slap him around. He soon learned hiding in his room or hanging out in the streets with his Lebanese buddies was safer.

Over the years, the men kept coming, and Umair kept to the streets. His mom was never around to check on him because she labored away as a waitress in a local Lebanese diner for dollar tips. However, one thing that remained constant in his life was his friends, who shared his contempt for staying home or going to school. They were tough kids who soon ruled Warren Avenue, the main drag through Dearborn, Michigan. When he was sixteen, Umair formed a gang—more for group identification than criminal activity. That would come later. He designed the gang insignia they wore on their backs depicting a shamshir sword underlying their name: "Warren Bros."

Needing to raise some cash to support their growing band, they looked to the reliable street business of selling dope. Aware that a white gang was selling drugs along Warren Avenue, Umair, and his crew gathered information using surveillance and the purchase of drugs to get an idea of how much money was involved. It was a lot. They decided it was time to act.

At first, Warren Bros sold methamphetamine and opioids. As they expanded, the Bros began banging heads with the other gang, who made it clear they were not wanted in the area by beating one of the Bros nearly to death and leaving a note pinned to his pocket: "Stay off our turf."

Umair, with his lieutenants, decided to strike back. On a hot, humid Saturday night in August, at precisely nine p.m., the Warren Bros attacked five of the gang's drug dealers—beating them, taking their dope, money, and weapons—and raced to Crowley Park, where they prepared for part two of the plan.

Acting swiftly, the gang members assembled at the dark end of the park, where they had been involved in drug dealing activities for several months. They devised a plan, with Umair volunteering to be a decoy. The gang leader positioned himself in a known meeting spot for drug users, anticipating the inevitable confrontation. Meanwhile, ten other members of the Warren Bros, armed with handguns and improvised weapons, strategically positioned themselves, fully aware that the gang would come around seeking revenge.

The plan was simple enough. When the gangbangers got out of their cars, the Bros would jump them and beat them up. Just twenty minutes after setting up, the gang saw a lowered Chevy with its lights out slowly approaching. As the car drew near Umair, it veered to the left, and just as quickly, two people began shooting at Umair from the right side of the vehicle from thirty feet away. Suddenly, the sound of gunfire with blinding flashes filled the night, destroying everyone's hearing and night vision. Umair was prepared, pulled his gun, and fired back at the flashes, as did five of his protectors. After ten seconds of ear-piercing clamor, the only sound was the Chevy accelerating from the location, heading toward Warren Avenue.

Still blinded, several Bros ran towards where Umair had been standing and finally located him under a parked car. He looked lifeless. As they dragged him from under the car, they saw blood splattered all over and thankfully heard Umair moaning. Most of these young kids had never been shot or had seen what bullets do to a body. Two of the kids puked right on the spot. The ones who could still function grabbed Umair put him in one of the cars and got him out of the area as sirens could be heard in the distance, approaching fast.

Umair had prepared for this situation. One of the group had a brother, Omar, who had chosen to pursue a higher education as a pre-med student rather than live on the streets fighting. If anyone ever got shot, Omar had promised to help. Taking Umair to Omar's house, the guys unloaded him to the basement, where a makeshift emergency room was set up. Omar went to work. Fortunately, his work was easily manageable, as the hole in Umair's upper right leg was a through-and-through wound. After sewing up the two holes, Omar said it was best he spent at least one night recovering in the basement. All agreed.

With Umair asleep and things quieting down, several Bros were checking their phones to see what was happening with the cops. That didn't take long as the headlines on the Dearborn Times-Herald website announced:

Gang Shooting - One Dead, Three Wounded

By Times-Herald Newspapers

> Late this evening, Dearborn police responded to Crowley Park after a report of gunfire. Upon arriving, officers found evidence of a shooting but no suspects in the area. At about the same time, a second DPD unit observed a Chevy driving at a high rate of speed down Wheeler Avenue with its lights off. Officers stopped the vehicle and found the front passenger dead from what appeared to be a bullet wound and three others seriously wounded. The three victims were taken by ambulance to Beaumont Hospital, where their condition has not been reported. The driver of the car was arrested. Police stated it appeared to be a gang-related shooting. No further details were provided.

In court a year later, two Warren Bros gang members, both seventeen, were depicted as two innocent victims walking home when the other gang members attacked them. While the court ruled they should not have been carrying guns, the defense substantiated how dangerous the area was, and they needed to be able to protect themselves. Ultimately, the surviving three gang members, along with their leader and driver, were sentenced to eight years in prison, eliminating all competition for the Bros on Warren Street. The two Lebanese kids were found guilty of one count of manslaughter and sentenced to two years in juvenile hall. They were both out in a year and a half. There was never any mention of Umair. As time passed, Umair went from selling drugs with a plan of running guns. His meeting at the mosque was his first move.

Chapter 5

FBI Field Office

Detroit, Michigan

As he waited on the 26th floor of one of the tallest office buildings in Detroit for his partner, Harley Jennings couldn't help but reflect on his diverse career moves over the past five years. Hell, he thought, it was just five years ago he was fighting the Chinese on Woody Island as the PLA fought for the reunification of Taiwan. His heroic fighting as a Master Gunnery Sergeant in the Marine Corps earned him the Silver Star for his actions. Not a "hardware" type of guy, but it still meant a lot to the now-retired soldier. His thoughts drifted back to his youth.

Harley grew up in Douglas, Wyoming, a small town of sixty-three hundred that, like it or not, is known for the mythical creature called a jackalope, part rabbit and part antelope, a weird-looking bunny with antlers. Always one who liked to mix it up, the six foot two, 210-pounder played middle linebacker at Douglas High School all four years and, in his senior year, the team lost the 3A state championship to Buffalo 21-20. He was still pissed about that one.

Not wanting to follow in his father's footsteps as a deputy sheriff with Converse County, the barely eighteen-year-old enlisted in the Marine Corps. This was just after 9/11, and Harley prayed the conflicts in the Middle East wouldn't end before he could get there. He wanted payback.

Harley was right at home, spending most of his career in tanks. As a Marine, he valued the *esprit de corps* and the camaraderie. But after twenty years serving his country, he was ready for new challenges.

Harley's phone chirped, breaking into his thoughts. It was a text from Ali: "Sorry, man. My little one decided to take a big one, and I have diaper watch. Be there shortly." Some things never change. If this dude were ever on time, Harley would have to interrogate him to see why.

Putting his phone down, Harley recalled sitting on the back porch one summer night, sipping a beer with his dad. "Son, I know it must be tough deciding what to do with your life now. Hell, you're just thirty-eight with chapter two waiting to be written. I'm no author, but I have a suggestion I've been kicking around."

Harley glanced over his beer at his dad, who had all his attention, "Yeah, Dad, but no, I'm not going to be a county cop in Wyoming chasing jackalopes."

His Dad came back quickly, "Come on, son, hear me out on this one."

He took a big hit from his beer and said, "Sure, Dad, I'm listening."

"Good," his dad said, not revealing how happy he was that his son wanted to hear what he had to say. "Years ago, I became close friends with an FBI agent from the Casper field office when we were working together on a case involving some yahoos who decided to blow up the power plant here in Douglas. You weren't here then, but we didn't get the lights back on for nearly a week. Anyway, we got to talking, and he told me he was part of the Bureau's Counterterrorism Division. The war stories he told sure sounded more fun than what I was doing, that's for sure. Once—"

"Okay, Dad, the point."

"Sorry, son, I got carried away. I just got to thinking about how you might still like taking down terrorists now that you aren't shooting at them anymore. *Capische*?"

That took Harley aback. Wow, he had never thought of that—the FBI, terrorists, working as a team again... sounds good, he thought.

"What's wrong, son, no interest?"

"Sorry, Dad, it really sounds interesting. I'll check it out, that's for sure. I promise." They tapped their beers together in agreement.

Harley soon discovered that joining the FBI is about as tricky as being chosen as a Marine tank commander. After twenty years in the Corps, he knew about paperwork and all the bullshit and hoops you must jump through to be accepted. But if bureaucracy stopped many FBI recruits, Harley would not be one of them.

His first hurdle was his age. Anyone over thirty-seven could only apply with proof of being a military veteran; good old form DD-214 solved that. The next toughie was that applicants must have at least a bachelor's degree and two years of related work experience. Fortunately, Harley received college credit for certain Marine-related classes he took, and the rest he managed to complete over several years to obtain his BA degree. He was told his experience in the Marines was more than enough for the work experience requirement.

Next, Harley took several tests and more interviews; he passed the physical fitness test but would later admit that the 1.5-mile run almost did him in. Next up was another written test and an interview with a panel of special agents who seemed very interested in his combat experience during the Chinese American war.

After passing the initial phases of the application, Harley took a second physical and was told what great shape he was in. A polygraph examination and credit check followed this. Agents interviewed many of those he worked with in the Marines, even asking questions around Douglas. When the Bureau added ten points for being a veteran, he received a phone call that changed chapter two of his book forever—he was now cleared for the FBI academy.

Twenty years after completing basic training at Camp Pendleton, Harley quickly discerned he wasn't eighteen anymore. The twenty-week FBI course was intensive. The physical fitness training was tough, especially alongside the kids who took to calling him gramps. But while he couldn't run for shit, he kicked ass with push-ups and sit-ups. Not many recruits could match the numbers Harley put up.

In the classroom, Harley held his own, but it was a class on counterterrorism that grabbed his interest. Toward the end of the course, he applied for the Counterterrorism Division and was accepted. He was assigned to the Detroit field office, where he was now awaiting the ever-tardy Ali.

Chapter 6

FBI Field Office

Detroit, Michigan

As he checked his phone for the umpteenth time, Harley looked up and saw Ali prancing down the hall with his usual shit-eating grin. "Glad you could make it," Harley said sarcastically.

"Dude," replied Ali, "if you would ever marry and have a kid, you would see what a tough assignment it is."

"Have some coffee; it's only been sitting for an hour."

"Sometimes I wonder," said Ali, pouring himself a coffee, "how I managed to get such a nice guy as a partner."

"Okay, let's cut the bullshit and get down to business," Harley said with a smile. "First, I just got back the ID on our local gang banger. His name is Umair Sabar. Our intelligence says he leads a well-organized Muslim gang called the Warren Bros, who hang out at the dive, Tip a Few, over in Dearborn, which a Lebanese guy owns."

"Yeah, I know the place," said Ali, "it's a dump for sure, but has a hell of a collection of shamshir swords."

Just then, the Special Agent in Charge, or SAC, John Williamson, popped his head into the small conference room.

"Howdy. You guys working on that meet and greet the other day at the Muslim Center?"

"Sure are, boss," said Harley. "We got some ID on one of the suspects and are coming up with a plan of action."

"Great, keep me in the loop," said the SAC as he continued down the hall.

"Well, I guess," said Ali, "it looks like we got the brass's attention on this one."

"As we should," replied Harley. "When a known gang member talks with a probable Hezbollah terrorist, that's not good. The question staring us in the face is why."

"Agreed, what else do you have on—what did you say his name was?"

"Sabar. Umair Sabar," said Harley. "NCIC came back with very little. The guy is pretty clean, just some minor shit not amounting to anything. The only item of interest is a shooting that occurred a few years ago between the Warren Bros and a gang from Detroit over drug turf. One member of the Detroit gang was killed, and three others were hit but survived. Two Warren gang members got a slap on the wrist and basically skated on this one. Other than that, nothing."

"So," Ali said, "what should our next move be?"

"I suggest we put surveillance on him for a few days and see what he is up to—where he goes, who he's talking to, and whether he makes a move to meet up with Mr. Hezbollah. I'll run it by the SAC."

"Sounds good," said Ali. "What about Mr. Hezbollah, anything?"

"That's the strange thing," exclaimed Harley, "nothing came back on this guy. But a man running around with security does not fit the pattern of someone from the mosque. I would bet he is a terrorist and, for some reason, needs the help of the Warren Bros gang. What do you think, we put him under surveillance also?"

"I agree; we need to get a handle on this before the shit hits the fan—and with these circumstances, it sure seems possible."

"I'm on it," said Harley as he got up and headed back to his desk, wondering where this was going.

Chapter 7

Imam Ali Military Base

Abu Ahmad, Syria

Located on the Syrian border with Iraq, Imam Ali Garrison was where American Ahmad Nadar began his advanced terrorist training. In everything he did, everywhere he went, he was cautious about keeping his identity and mission secret. On most trips, Ahmad had a black hood covering his head. He was never told who his instructors were or the names of others taking part in the training with him. He could talk with no one. At times, he felt like an army of one, and other times, like a prisoner. He never felt any camaraderie. But he was learning the ways of a terrorist, and he embraced it.

After two months of initial training, Ahmad was chosen for the elite Quds Force, similar to the SEALs or Delta Force in his spurned country. The Quds is a highly skilled unit specializing in unconventional warfare, special operations, and military intelligence. The force is under the direct command of the Supreme Leader of Iran. The US and other democratic countries have designated it a foreign terrorist organization.

Ahmad's Quds training made his earlier drills seem like a walk in the park. Now, exercises were done in units of two, with no one pair knowing the other pair. All activities were done independently, and the two men were not allowed to talk to each other unless it was directly related to their mission. They were monitored closely. Housing was also segregated for each person. There was no interaction whatsoever.

One aspect of Ahmad's training was shoulder-fired weaponry, specifically the M72, using different ammunition against various targets, including reinforced steel and brick structures. Ahmad noted that he received more training on this weapon than any other, except rifles and handguns. He was too busy to wonder why.

Ahmad was moved around Iran to different garrisons for themes such as survival training, practical missile training, bomb-making, urban training, high-speed driving with both cars and motorcycles, commando training, and tactical training. He had classes on guerilla tactics and clandestine missions on foreign soil, using several countries as examples, including the United States. He learned how to operate with two-man squads or, at other times, up to ten. When he operated with larger teams, he was always placed in charge.

During his last weeks of training, Ahmad was assigned to Unit 910 of the Quds, tasked with external operations in Israel and abroad. At the end of his training, he felt confident he could handle any assignment—and succeed.

Chapter 8

Office of the Supreme Leader

Tehran, Islamic Republic of Iran

As the Supreme Leader of Iran, Amir Massad looked around his elegant office and into the faces of his ruling elite. He knew as they did that these clerics would carry out his every word—or they would be dead. That was how he ruled.

Since 2021, the relatively young Massad had set policies for his country as the commander-in-chief of the armed forces and as the head of the intelligence and security operations, deciding where the focus of his Islamic regime would be. Massad could appoint or dismiss the judiciary leaders, the state radio and television networks, and the powerful Islamic Revolutionary Guard Corps commander. He alone could declare war or peace.

Massad appointed six of the Council of Guardians, the all-encompassing body overseeing Parliament's actions, giving him control over which nominees could run for public office.

Additionally, Massad ensured his power reached to all corners of Iran. This was achieved by placing eighteen hundred representatives, or, as some would whisper, spies, spread throughout the country. They were placed in all government segments and served as his emissaries, reporting on anyone who might question his authority.

"I want to call this meeting to order," said the Supreme Leader. "I realize we all know each other, but we have some new faces from the National Security and Intelligence Division, so I want to go around the table and have each person introduce themselves and say something about what they do. I will be the exception. General, let's start with you."

"Thank you, Supreme Leader. I'm Mohammad Khodadadi, chief of the General Staff tasked with coordinating activities within the armed forces." Then, the Eyes shifted to the next person at the table.

"Thank you, Your Majesty. I'm Farhad Amin, the president of our beloved country, and I do whatever I can to assist our Supreme Leader."

"Hello, I'm Bahman Mahmoud, speaker of the Parliament, whose 290 members serve our Supreme Leader."

The head of the judiciary, the ministers of foreign affairs, the interior and intelligence, and the Islamic

Revolutionary Guard Corps commander, Arman Ahmadzadeh, also introduced themselves.

"Thank you for coming together today. As you can see by the agenda, our council must decide what action to take against the American infidels and the axis of resistance for the continual unprovoked killing of our brothers, this time Major General Foroohar Nakhjevani and Kourosh Ormazd. And lest we forget, the airstrike that killed General Qassem Soleimani just a few years earlier. We all belong to Allah, and to Him, we will return. Praise Allah to guide them to Paradise.

The room promptly answered back, “Praise Allah.”

"These killings of our leaders must stop. Our enemies constantly accuse us of human rights abuses and anti-Western ideology. But it's not just that. Since our success with the lawful taking of the US hostages in 1979 and our triumphant revolution, the Americans have sabotaged our nuclear program. Since 1995, they have choked us with an embargo." Glancing around the room, Amir saw he had everyone's undivided attention, and continued.

"The security of our country is critical to our survival. Without question, the US and their cronies, the Saudis and Israelis, are determined to plot a regime change and insert a puppet government in our place. We must use the Syrian civil war to create opportunities for ourselves." Standing up to deliver his final remark, he raised his voice to a crescendo, "It's time we take the war to our enemies at a time of our choosing and become the single power in the Middle East." Everyone in the room jumped up impulsively, clapping and shaking their fist violently in agreement with their Supreme Leader. When everyone took their seats, Amir laid out his detailed plan to strike the United States.

Chapter 9

Islamic Revolutionary Guard Corps

Beirut, Lebanon

Ahmad completed his training with no fanfare, no graduation, no nothing. The one positive was he no longer had to wear a black hood over his head. The confident, newly produced terrorist was secretly transported to Lebanon and IRGC headquarters in Beirut.

Waiting outside some big office by himself, he sat across from a prominent sign that read:

"Prepare Against Them Whatever You Are Able of Power"

After a half-hour of waiting, he was shown into a large, well-decorated room consisting of mostly military slogans and memorabilia. Only one man was in the office, neatly dressed in an Iranian army major general's uniform.

As he approached the desk, General Arman Ahmadzadeh came around to greet him by extending his hand to shake. "Salam."

"Salam, Major General."

After they were seated, the commanding general of IRGC said, "I understand you completed your training, and

I must say you performed beyond our expectations, bettering some men we knew would perform highly.

"Yes, I always drive myself hard and set high goals. My belief in Allah makes me a stronger person, Major General. Mashallah."

"Ahmad, your name has been discussed at the highest levels of our government. We have a highly classified mission for which we have chosen you. You will learn more about it as we proceed. First, we want you to take up residence in Dearborn, Michigan, which, as you know, is a prominent Muslim city in the heart of the US. Once there, we will put you in contact with a group of like-minded men who will help you in our holy battle. Do you have any questions?"

"No, General Ahmadzadeh, my will is to serve Allah in any way I can. The Qur'an leads me. 'Permission to fight is given to those against whom fighting is launched because they have been wronged.'"

"Good," said the general. "You will fly to the United States. Your cover story is that you traveled around Europe on a long backpacking vacation before beginning your professional life as an apprentice electrician in Dearborn. You are moving from Mississippi to be a self-sufficient Muslim and better yourself in the eyes of Allah. Pack your belongings, as you will leave tonight. May Allah guide and protect you in our holy war against those who would harm our country. Khoda-Hafez."

Chapter 10

Beirut, Lebanon

As he threw his duffle bag in the back of the pickup truck, Ahmad Nadar was happy he didn't have to wear a black hood. That's progress, he thought. He and his driver, who only gave his name as Ibrahim, were wearing civilian clothes; for what, he was not sure. He did know he was supposed to be heading for the US, but how he would get there was once again kept secret. One thing about these Iranians is that they don't talk much.

Ahmad broke the silence. "So, my brother, where are we headed together?"

"I was told the less you know, the better for us both." He handed Ahmad a packet, "Here is your American passport, some cash, and the wallet you came here with. We will have to pass through some checkpoints, so I want to ensure you are prepared. I will ask you questions similar to what you will be asked at the checkpoints." As Ibrahim said this, Ahmad noticed they were heading north on Route 51, which, as he recalled from his map training, ran north and south along the Mediterranean Sea.

Ibrahim wasted no time. "Mr. Nadar, what brings you here to Syria all the way from the United States?"

"Salam," said Ahmad, "I'm here on vacation, visiting my ancestral country of Lebanon, and now we are headed to Turkey."

"Do you have guns or drugs in the car?"

"No, I don't believe in those things, as I'm a man of God."

"I don't think you need to add that," said Ibrahim. "Don't volunteer any information; just answer yes or no to their questions."

"Got it."

As it happened, the two men went through several checkpoints in Syria and Turkey with no problems. The guards bought into Ahmad's story of his vacation to his homeland. It helped that he spoke fluent Arabic, even though most guards spoke English.

Ahmad caught some shut-eye during the fifteen-hour drive to Antalya, Turkey, and even switched off with Ibrahim when he became too tired to drive. It was all working out.

Arriving at Antalya Airport in Turkey, Ibrahim handed Ahmad a packet containing tickets for his flight from Antalya to Athens, Greece, then to London, England, and finally to John F. Kennedy International Airport in New York City.

After flying for over a day, Ahmad learned the true meaning of jet lag. He felt beat up and tired while excited for his yet-to-be-announced mission in what was now his renounced country.

Ahmad felt transformed as he boarded his final flight to Jackson-Evers International Airport in Mississippi. While he had become accustomed to Lebanon and Iran, he felt somewhat alien here in the United States, like he didn't belong—nothing new. However, because he was now traveling as a skilled Hezbollah terrorist belonging to Quds special forces, he found comfort in knowing he was more than ready physically and mentally for whatever Allah would have him do.

After going through the motions with his parents, just briefly telling them of his "vacation," Ahmad slept for two days and then was off to Dearborn, driving a used black Ford sedan he had just purchased. As he was ordered to do, Ahmad bought a KryptAll phone, which uses a unique network of secure servers that allows 256-bit AES encrypted calls through more than one hundred interconnection points. Soon after hitting Interstate 55 for his fourteen-hour drive,

Ahmad received a text with directions to an address in Dearborn and entry codes for the garage and house.

Arriving at 9:00 p.m., Ahmad used the electronic codes to park his car in the garage and enter the well-furnished home. This would be his new residence, a modest single-family home with a sizeable two-stall garage. It was located in a predominately Muslim middle-class neighborhood. As he checked out his new digs, he saw it even had his favorite foods stocked in the refrigerator and on the cabinet shelves. He went to bed with no new orders, hoping his mission would begin soon.

Chapter 11

Muslim Center of Michigan

Dearborn, Michigan

Within the concealed depths of the 130,000-square-foot Muslim Center of Michigan, MCOM, a Shia Mosque, a hidden abode, provided seclusion for the giant and the man entrusted to his protection. Shielded from the view of those both within and outside the mosque, they found themselves adjusting to their new surroundings as recent additions to the community. The manager was told by the director of an analogous mosque in Lebanon that the men were politically influential and were reviewing the center to bring their mosque more in line with the success of others.

Samir Makhlouf, a high-ranking cleric, was hand-picked and sent to Dearborn on the order of the Supreme Leader. The giant, Mustafa Latif, was a Quds soldier from the Islamic Revolutionary Guard, specially trained for personal protection. Samir understood his mission would be crucial to the revolution. He was being sent directives covertly for step-by-step actions.

Sitting at his small desk, Makhlouf reviewed new orders he had just received:

You are to meet our agent, Ahmad, at the basement entrance at 0300 hours. At that time, you both will receive further instructions.

At 0250 hours, Makhlouf and Latif were waiting at the rear basement entrance. At precisely 0300, there was a light tap on the small wooden door. Latif carefully opened it and saw a man dressed in all black staring at him.

"I'm Ahmad."

As Ahmad stepped into the entrance and into the light, Makhlouf blurted out, "You're American!"

Stopping in his tracks, Ahmad glared at the cleric and said, "Yes, and that is the last time you or anyone else will refer to my nationality. I'm a man of God, here to further the revolution in the name of Bilad Faris and Allah."

"You can't talk to me like that," said an obviously agitated Makhlouf.

Ahmad took a step closer toward Makhlouf, causing Latif to move in to separate them. "Where to?" Ahmad sharply asked. Makhlouf pointed to his desk.

Once inside the residence, Makhlouf sat behind his small desk, which seemed all the smaller with Latif's presence. Ahmad sat next to him but slightly in front. There was silence as the three men sized each other up.

Makhlouf spoke first. "I think we need to make something clear right from the start. The Supreme Leader chose me to run this operation, and my position demands your utmost respect."

"And it will be my ass on the front lines making sure we are all successful, so I ask that you show me the respect I deserve."

Just then, their identical phones beeped. The phone screens illuminated both men's faces as they each read their text message:

Before proceeding to the next phase, we want Ahmad to befriend the leader of a local Lebanese street gang called the Warren Bros. The leader's name is Umair Sabar, a Lebanese native who hangs out at a bar named Tip a Few. We think he could be of help to us. Be careful in what you reveal to get his cooperation; it may take some time, which we have allowed for. Samir, stay out of the public eye as we have information the FBI is watching the mosque closely. Support Ahmad in anything he needs. Praise be to Allah and your mission.

"You have my number if you need me," said Ahmad. And with that, he was up and out the back door. Outside the mosque, two FBI agents staked out under a tree in their nondescript car failed to detect the man dressed in black as he crossed the parking lot. It didn't help that both men were on the nod. In the morning, they would report to FBI headquarters that no unusual activity was detected.

Chapter 12

USS *Ford* - Carrier Strike Group 12

Arabian Sea

Nervously walking, almost sprinting between the bridge and the combat information center, CIC, and finally on the flag bridge, Captain Dick "Mad Dog" Johnson the CAG the Commander Air Wing 8, was concerned about his "kids" taking part in a major exercise involving his F-35s escorting four B-52H Stratofortress aircraft across the Middle East.

US Central Command, or USCENTCOM, controlled the exercise, which also involved two Israeli Air Force F-35 Adir fighter jets. Bahrain, Qatar, and Saudi Arabia were providing support for the flyovers. The show of force, mainly for Iran's benefit, demonstrated the quickness with which America's allies can bring overwhelming combat power to the region.

"Dick," said the CO, Captain Otis C. Albright, "this isn't a battle against China; that was five years ago. Relax; no one is shooting at us."

"I hate not being there with them," said Mad Dog. "When I have no real control of my pilots, I just worry like

I'm their mom or something." Barely finishing his sentence, he took off for the CIC.

Over the Persian Gulf, hugging the shoreline of Saudi Arabia, radio chatter picked up when the flight leader, Lieutenant Commander Jessie Hampton, sounded an alarm. "Control, Boxer 11, we are being lit up by Iranian land-based tracking radar. No targeting radar at this time."

"Boxer 11, Control, do not target their radar source. Stay on course with the big boys."

"Control, Boxer 11, roger." To say the flight commander had an itchy trigger finger would be an understatement. One of the best pilots to ever come out of flight training school, Jessie always liked to prove it. During the war with China, Jessie mixed it up with a J-20 and was shot down, punching out at the last second. It seemed like he was always looking for the pilot who managed to do that, just to even the score. But in the five years since Jessie had only trained and trained. He wanted more, but today would not be that day.

Back on board the USS *Ford*, catching the third arresting wire like the excellent pilot he was, Jessie headed for the Ready Room for a debrief. The first person he saw was the CAG. "How'd it go out there?" Mad Dog asked.

"Great, sir; I just wish those assholes would have shown some balls and challenged us instead of only using their ground-based radar."

"Well, that's what a peacetime Navy is like," said the CAG. "Don't worry; I've got a sneaking suspicion our time will come from those arrogant bastards from Iran."

"Roger that, sir, we can only hope so. That's how we ride." Putting his gear away, Jessie couldn't wait for that day. He just wanted it to happen before he rotated back to the States. He had something to prove.

Chapter 13

Tip a Few

Dearborn, Michigan

Leaving their office on Michigan Avenue in Detroit, FBI agents Harley Jennings and Ali Mohsen were dressed like the dirtbag gangbangers they were about to eavesdrop on.

With Harley driving the rented Ford F150 like a tank, Ali couldn't hold back. "What the heck, Harley, have you ever figured out you are no longer in the Marines driving an Abrams? You've got to relax your grip on the steering wheel and pretend you are driving a brand-new Ford truck—because you are!"

"Some gunner you are. If you'd learn to relax, it wouldn't feel like my old M1, which by the way, could haul ass, not like this gutless wonder."

"Okay," said Ali, giving up, "let's go over our plans again; we're almost there."

"Like I said," exclaimed Harley as he seemed to hit every rut on Warren Avenue without noticing. "We are two buds working for UPS who decided we've had enough of the big city and are moving up to the Upper Peninsula. We are staying at Motel 6 across the street. The rest of the story we can bullshit through."

Like most undercover officers, neither was armed except with a knife. Ali was packing a William Henry titanium A200-3B and Harley, some cheap piece of shit that a Boy Scout would be embarrassed to own. He mostly carried it to open mail or clean his fingernails. The ex-Marine felt confident in his ability to kick ass anyplace, anytime. Who needed a knife?

As they pulled up to Tip a Few, they saw that most of the bulbs were burned out of the once bright neon sign. It now read "p a Few." Scanning the parking lot, they saw the truck they were most interested in, a raised red Dodge Ram with oversized off-road tires. That behemoth belonged to their man, Umair Sabar, who had gone calling on a probable Hezbollah terrorist, and they wanted to know why. Like breaking a huddle in a football game where the team claps their hands in unison, they simultaneously jumped from the Ford, whispering, "Let's do this."

As they walked in, the two undercover FBI agents felt the eyes of the entire tavern focus on them. They grabbed two seats at the bar, with a clear view of the beautiful shamshir swords. Harley ordered a beer while Ali chose a

Coke. A few minutes later, another stranger, Ahmad Nadar, entered and sat at the end of the bar.

Sitting in his usual booth in the back with two of his associates, Umair Sabar noticed the two men he had never seen before. While not unusual, as new blood came and went, they looked too polished for his liking. As Umair contemplated the situation and considered his best approach, a second, considerably younger Lebanese man entered the scene. While the man was unfamiliar to Umair, something about him suggested a toughness. Inexplicably, Umair felt a connection and was drawn to him. There was a certain resemblance to himself that he couldn't quite pinpoint, but it resonated with him.

Without saying anything to his buddies, Umair got up from the booth, carrying his longneck Almaza, and approached the polished guys. His two cohorts followed but stayed back a few feet. Like in some old movie, Umair said, "So, what brings you two into a place like this?"

Umair was standing nearest Harley, who answered first. "Well, my friend, if it's any of your business, we are staying across the street at the Motel 6 and decided we needed a drink—over."

Looking at Ali, the gang leader asked, "Why are you hanging with this bad-mannered white dude?"

"Excuse me?" said Ali. "Are you writing a book or something? Look, man, we don't want any trouble; we are two humble UPS drivers heading to the UP to get out of dives like this. We figure there must be something better out there. So why don't you piss off and leave us to our drinks."

Ahmad, taking this all in, understood it was Umair he was directed to befriend. He joined in, surprising everyone. "Look, guys, I don't think you fit this place either; I suggest you get out of here while you still can."

"Fuck me," said Harley, "I'm the only white dude in this dive, but you know what, I could give a shit."

After he took a long pull on his beer, Umair reached over and smacked Harley's beer from his hand. The mug went flying over the bar, smashing a shit load of glasses and spraying broken shards everywhere. The bartender yelled, "You better stop, or I'll call the police." That warning came too late.

Harley leaped from his seat, driving his head up and under Umair's chin, sending him backward into the arms of his two comrades. At that moment, Ahmad jumped from his seat and threw a wild right that Ali managed to duck, receiving only a glancing blow to his head. Ali quickly jumped on Ahmad, knocking him backward to the ground.

As he smacked Ahmad in the face, someone hit Ali on the back of his head. One moment, Ali was pounding on Ahmad; the next, he saw only black and slumped over Ahmad, out cold. Hearing sirens, the terrorist quickly pushed the man off him, headed for the back door, and jumped into his car, driving in the opposite direction of the approaching authorities.

With Umair out of action, Harley went after the two other men, who were more concerned with their boss than paying attention to Harley. He pounded the closest punk with a right that sent him backward, hitting his head on the edge of a table, spraying the area with blood. As Harley was going for the other man, several gangbangers jumped him and pinned him to the floor. As the fight continued, two Dearborn police officers came rushing through the front door, yelling, "Stop—police, everyone up against the bar with your hands behind your head—NOW." The room went silent for a moment as everyone debated their next move. When two more cops came rushing in from the back, everyone did as they were told.

The officers interviewed the bartender and some of the patrons separately, including Ali, who was having trouble remembering what had happened. Harley filled in the blank spots. When the officers were satisfied, three gang members were handcuffed along with Ahmad and Harley and transported to jail on assault charges. They all traveled in separate police cars.

When finally alone with the officers, Harley spoke up. "Listen, guys, I'm sorry about what happened, but I want you to know Mohsen and I are undercover FBI agents working a case. I need you to call the night supervisor at our FBI field office in Detroit. Here is the number.

"You guys," said the passenger officer, "sure have a strange way to operate—a bar fight."

"I know I sound like a kid at recess on the school playground," said Harley, "but they started it. We tried to be cool and get the shit we needed, but they jumped us. But listen, I need you guys to treat us like assholes, rough us up a bit if necessary, when the gangbangers can see it, so we keep our cover. Any problem with that?"

"No problem, that's the first thing you said that makes sense."

Harley got it going during booking as the group was in line to be fingerprinted. When the officer said to give him his right hand, Harley stated, "Fuck you guys, no way; my prints are already in the system."

The officer hesitated and then called over the jailer. The muscle-bound civilian efficiently grabbed Harley's left hand and bent it up behind his back as the officer grabbed Harley's right hand. The pain was excruciating. Harley grimaced and put on an award-winning show for the gang members. When it was over, the two agents were in their cell, out of sight of the gang members, and were released to another agent. A different FBI agent picked up the rented Ford and drove it back to headquarters. As Harley drove home late that night, he knew he would have a ton of explaining to do at work the next day—but what's new, he thought.

Chapter 14

Dearborn, Michigan

Waiting for two days after the fight at Tip a Few, Ahmad had Umair's cell phone number and thought he should text him. He felt an internal urgency to get this mission going no matter what he heard from his handlers.

This is Ahmad. I was at the bar two nights ago and want to talk to you. Is there a place we could meet besides your hangout?

After about two minutes, he got a reply from Umair.

When I met with Samir, he suggested someone important would contact me. He didn't give me your name. How about Crowley Park in an hour?

See you then.

Ahmad arrived at the park first and found a picnic table to sit on. Umair came a few minutes later. Ahmad stood up to welcome Umair in Arabic, "Assalamu alaikum," as he extended his hand to Umair, who repeated the welcome.

"I didn't know who you were at the time," said Umair, "but thanks for helping out at the bar the other night."

Sitting back down on the picnic table, Ahmad said, "I didn't like those guys either, especially the white guy. They should know better than to come crashing into a Lebanese bar. Although I will say that the Middle Eastern guy got me on the ground and started to whale on me until one of your guys smacked him over the head with an Almaza. It was my bad; I missed my first punch."

"Yeah, I see you have a shiner going there."

"A mark for my miscalculation from which I learn quickly," said Ahmad.

"So, what is your interest in me?" asked Umair.

Ahmad replied, "Umair, I believe we have much in common; please tell me about your Lebanese heritage. I would guess you are as proud of that as I am of mine."

Umair told of his life since being born in Lebanon, his troubles at home with a mom who was never there, how he started the Warren Bros gang, and how they were his only true friends. Umair couldn't even hold back telling Ahmad how much money they were making handling the drug trafficking in his part of the city.

"Listen, my brother, I want to tell you about my gang, Hezbollah." Ahmad spent the next half hour explaining to Umair their ideology, knowing Umair would relate to it. He described their beginnings when Ayatollah Ruhollah Khomeini, leader of Shiite radicalism, spread the Islamic Revolution in 1982 after the Israel invasion. Ahmad told him how Hezbollah's ideology is to expel Americans, the French, and all their allies from Lebanon and that they are one of the principal resistance groups in the Middle East to use tactics of suicide bombing and assassinations.

Ahmad went on to explain how Hezbollah is losing its grip on Lebanon. "There is an increase in independent and anti-establishment politicians dissatisfied with the group and other longtime power holders. They are seeking change. Some in the country even want to disarm Hezbollah, voicing their concerns that they can no longer defend Lebanon. Many, like me, feel it's time to alter these misconceptions and for us to strike back at the Americans and Israelis to demonstrate the strength of Hezbollah. That is our goal and our plan.

"Are you suggesting," said Umair, "for me to somehow help you in your plans against the US? I have so much going on with my brothers; I don't know."

"No problem. Let's talk some more. Let me send you some information about Hezbollah, what we are trying to do in the world, and why our mission is so important." Umair nodded as the two headed to their cars. As he drove off, Ahmad thought his first face-to-face meeting with Umair went well. Now, he must find out just what mission he will lead.

Chapter 15

FBI Field Office

Detroit, Michigan

The Special Agent in Charge, John Williamson, was not happy as he stared intensely at Harley and Ali with his penetrating blue eyes. "What were you thinking, getting into a bar fight with the one man we are trying to see what he is up to? Oh, excuse me, I said 'thinking,' my mistake. Which one of you dummies wants to explain your actions?"

The two agents looked at each other briefly, and then Harley took the lead. "Sir, it's on me. We were sitting at the bar when Umair approached us. We gave him our cover story, but the asshole got belligerent and knocked my beer out of my hand. Well, sir, that's when the Marine in me took over, and I charged the guy."

"The Marine in you? Come on, what happened to the professional FBI agent who thinks through these things so we don't blow a chance to see what he is up to? And who knows, perhaps even build rapport. What kind of lame excuse do you have, Ali?"

Ali stirred in his seat. "Sir, I don't remember much after I got hit over the head, but what Harley says is what happened. I don't know why they attacked us or who the guy was beside me, who seemed new to the place. Sir, I had to protect myself, so I fought back."

"Great, two highly trained field agents lose all control and handle a confrontation like two school kids taking on a bully at school. Come on, guys, really?"

"I will say this," said Harley, "We put on a good show while being booked and, just maybe, won some respect from Umair and his crew. I think it might be possible to try this again."

"What happened to the guy who attacked you, Ali?"

"As I said, I was out cold and—"

"Sir," said Harley, "the stranger took off through the back door like he was scared of something or someone. I don't think he is part of the gang, just another Lebanese punk coming in for a drink."

"But I will say this," said Ali, "the dude didn't look like just another dipshit; he seemed—more professional. Something about him stood out in the few minutes I had to check him out."

The SAC just stared at the two agents and wondered how his elite terrorist unit ended up fighting gangs instead of terrorists. They all needed to make some headway on this case. "Okay, let's get back to square one. We have a

Lebanese gang leader meeting with a possible Hezbollah terrorist at the mosque, and we need to find a connection. Thanks to you two, snooping around the bar didn't work, so I suggest we go back to surveillance. You have my permission to use whatever assets you need, but I need answers, not fights. Got it?"

Nodding their heads, both answered, "Yes, sir." They left the room with a little less ass.

Chapter 16

Dearborn, Michigan

Ahmad Nadar was now a highly trained Hezbollah terrorist and was anxious to fight. Although he didn't care much for the cleric sent by the Supreme Leader, he knew how to take orders and do as he was told. But there was no rule against pushing back a little. The more he thought about it, the more he convinced himself that it was difficult to operate without knowing the mission. He needed direction.

Ahmad dialed Samir, who was secluded at the Muslim Center of Michigan. Both lines were secure. Samir answered on the first ring. "Salam, glory be to Allah."

"Salam. And to Allah, praise be to the Creator of the universe."

"Samir," said Ahmad, "I call today with all respect for you and what you do for the revolution. I know it must be hard for you to deal with someone American. But I tell you, as Allah is my witness, I'm part American only because I was born here and I have an American mother. Lebanon, through my father, is my native land and what I would die for if necessary. I denounce any allegiance to the US."

"I understand your position quite well," said Samir. "Your name and mission have been discussed many times at the highest levels. And what you just said has been looked at closely, as you can imagine, all the way up to the Supreme Leader. You are the chosen one because we believe in you. We pray to Allah for your success—our success."

"Thank you to Allah and you, Samir," said Ahmad sincerely. “I have prayed for this and believe it is time to be told why I'm back in this country and what people expect of me."

"Yes, my brother," Samir said, showing respect to a half-Lebanese man and the sworn enemy of America. "I want you to continue your efforts to befriend Umair and keep me updated." There was a pause of a few seconds. "I wanted to do this in person but don't want to risk you coming here, as we believe we are being watched around the clock." Another pause and Ahmad wondered what was coming next. He didn't have to wait long.

"I have been in continual contact with my people in Iran and Lebanon, and all have agreed it's time to speak to you about the mission. Let me explain." Ahmad's heart skipped a beat as he anxiously awaited whatever they had for him. Samir continued, "The Americans kill our leaders, attack our nuclear programs, and harass us in our own country. There is a growing misconception that Hezbollah is not the power it once was. As he does in Allah, the Supreme Leader believes it is time to strike the Americans at the very heart and soul of their country."

"Yes, brother, and what might that be?"

"Independence Hall in Philadelphia is one of the most iconic symbols of freedom in the entire world. It's the same building where the Declaration of Independence and their US Constitution were debated and signed. Simply put, it is the birthplace of their nation."

Hearing this for the first time, Ahmad was speechless. Independence Hall, who would have thought? Hell, his mom made him go there during a vacation when he was like twelve. Even back then, he felt it didn't represent anything he believed in. A kid who was never accepted as an American but as some raghead from the Middle East could not relate to such a symbol—not then, not now, not ever.

"Praise be to Allah," said Ahmad, "may He give us the wisdom and power to succeed. I am ready for this mission, Samir, and take great pride in being the one chosen to lead the assault."

"We knew you would be. A reminder: Not a written word or a word spoken to anyone about it; this mission will only succeed if total secrecy is maintained. Now, work on getting Umair on our side. Goodbye." The line went silent, but not the beating of his heart—which Ahmad could hear as adrenaline flowed through his system—for something this big. He felt Allah brought him into the world for just this operation. Praise be to Allah; he wouldn't fail.

Chapter 17

Independence Hall

Philadelphia, Pennsylvania

After only working as a security guard at Independence Hall for less than a year, Kordell Jackson, a former Philadelphia police officer, had yet to get used to seeing Thomas Jefferson, John Adams, and Benjamin Franklin walking the halls. Getting to know the actors over the past months, he found it interesting that they never went out of character. You had to call them by their historical names. No exceptions.

It was about the only thing he found amusing. Leading up to this job, his life had become a shit show. Kordell had experienced how the human spirit can be torn apart by one event that can change you forever. One day, you are married with two girls and a wife who loves you—the next, you're not. No, he thought, I was a content street cop patrolling my native Philadelphia, doing the job I always wanted, until that night.

The memory of it played back like a movie on a continual loop. It was always in vivid color, and the ending never changed. No matter what he did or how he tried to change the tactics, his partner always ended up with a large bullet hole in the middle of his forehead, with eyes blankly staring back at him. Hearing him take his last breath, then hearing nothing was too much for his soul. In war, they call it post-traumatic stress disorder; in police work, they tell you to cowboy up, it wasn't your fault—you'll be fine. "Go get 'em, kid."

Now at "home" in his one-room apartment, with no kids and no wife, Kordell hit the rack, hoping the movie would not play tonight—but it always did.

"All units and 3511, robbery in progress at the liquor store, 261 W. Olney Avenue, Priority 1. Suspect last seen running eastbound, described as a white male, medium height and weight, wearing a black windbreaker and red skullcap."

"Shit," said Robbie, his probationary partner who had gotten out of the academy just five months earlier, "We're on Olney, and close."

It's always a cop's dream, a hot call: You look up, and you're right there. Picking up the mic, Robbie notified the dispatcher. "3511, we're in the area now."

"Roger 3511. All units, 3511 is in the area of the robbery suspect last seen running eastbound on Olney."

"3511, be advised, suspect is reportedly armed with a semi-automatic pistol."

"3511, roger."

Suddenly: "There he is," yelled Robbie, pointing at a man running and cutting down South 35th Drive just in front of them. Kordell floored his 2022 Dodge Durango, and the SUV responded, closing the gap to the suspect. They both saw him look over his shoulder as he turned the corner.

"3511, suspect spotted running south on 35th Drive."

"When we bail," yelled Kordell to his twenty-two-year-old partner, "we stick together, got it?"

"Stop," yelled Robbie. “He's cutting between those houses." Kordell slammed on the brakes, and Robbie was out of the SUV before it stopped. As the car screeched to a halt, Kordell was yelling for Robbie to wait, but instead, he heard him screaming, "Police—stop, or I'll shoot."

Kordell screamed into the mic, "3511, my partner is in foot pursuit, requesting assistance."

Running around the car, heading to where he last saw his partner, Kordell drew his Glock 19, turning on the specially mounted Streamlight. Then he heard it, a single shot penetrating the night stillness and echoing between the houses, sending a cold chill down his back. As he rounded the corner of the house, Kordell went about fifteen yards and spotted his partner on his back. He quickly flashed his light around the yard but didn't see anyone. He heard dogs barking from the house next door. He holstered his weapon as he slid to his knees beside Robbie. Blood from the bullet hole was trickling from Robbie's forehead, rolling down either side of his young face. His eyes were staring up at the sky, right past Kordell, seeing nothing. Then he heard the sound he would never forget as Robbie grunted out his last breath—then nothing. Kordell fell on him sobbing, "I told you to wait, I told you to wait, why didn't you wait?" When the first backup unit arrived, they found them; Kordell was still leaning over his partner, softly asking, "Why didn't you wait? Why?"

Kordell never recovered from his grief and guilt for not being there for his partner. His wife and two teenage girls did everything they could to snap him out of his depression, but their love was not strong enough to overcome his sorrow. As days turned into months, Kordell took to drinking. From the time he woke until he passed out at night, the movie and the depression never stopped. Nor did the drinking and the pills. The department ordered shrinks and mandatory therapy, but nothing helped. His old partners tried, and his family kept trying even though he was becoming belligerent towards them and often threatening. No one seemed able to penetrate his fog of despair.

One night, Kordell was running drunk around his home, brandishing his gun, yelling, "Stop, stop." When his wife tried to calm him, he pointed the gun at her and threatened to shoot. For him, it was the endless horror of the continuing movie and the need to prevent his partner from being shot—again and again.

After this episode, Kordell was fired from PPD, and his shrink committed him to a psychiatric facility. Soon after, his wife filed for divorce.

After four months of forced soberness in the facility, the fog of depression lessened. On many nights, the movie would not play. Kordell soon learned to cope with his depression and, with medication, was again becoming a functioning human being.

After several discussions with Kordell, a former partner, now retired, who ran security at Independence Hall convinced him to take the security guard position he had open. It was a low-stress job where his friend could still keep an eye on him and help him along his path to a new life. Kordell had even begun seeing his ex-wife again in public, although she brought one of her girlfriends along for help if needed. It wasn't. With a much clearer head on his shoulders,

Kordell was coming around. The movie seldom played anymore.

Chapter 18

Tip a Few

Dearborn, Michigan

Pulling up near Tip a Few in their nondescript silver Chevy, Harley picked a location farther away from the bar but still had clear eyes on the building. Both agents were getting ready for another dull stakeout. "This looks good," said Ali, "although I liked it better sitting at the bar sipping a Coke."

"Roger that," came back the reply. "But I tell you what"

"What?" interrupted Ali, smiling.

"If you would shut up, I'd tell you. If we keep drawing nothing from these stakeouts, I think we need to try the bar again. I mean, go inside and test the waters. If we see it starting to go sideways, we unass the area. Don't you think?"

"I'm for that," said Ali. "We've been working this case for a while and don't have shit to show for it. We need to turn the wick up a little."

At that moment, an older black Ford sedan pulled up in the back. Quickly, Ali grabbed his Nikon LaserForce Rangefinder binoculars from his lap and zeroed in on the man getting out. Harley started snapping photos with his

Canon EOS R7. "Dude, I think it's the same guy that smacked me in the bar—"

"You sure?"

Having eyes on for only a few seconds before the subject walked into the bar, Ali said "Yeah, that's him, I'm sure of it."

"Okay, I'm calling in our two backups so we can adequately surveil this prick when he leaves."

After making the necessary notifications and positioning the two additional units in the appropriate locations, it was back to the waiting game. "Here's what I think, Ali. We now have what I believe is another player. We know he has been to the bar at least twice now, which puts him on my radar. He could be another wannabe, or he could be more. And since I don't believe in coincidences, I'm thinking more."

"I agree," said Ali. "We have a Lebanese guy who comes to the bar and seems not to know anyone, given where he sits. He doesn't appear to be just another gangbanger, but something more."

Two hours later, the subject came out and went straight to his car. Using his portable radio, Ali put out the call, "One and Two, the subject is getting in his car; stand by for directions."

"Subject is turning right, eastbound on Warren. One, he's yours, we're following. Two, move ahead of us and stand by."

"One, he's turning southbound on Bingham—I think he's already on to us."

"One, pull off. Two, see if you can pick him up near Miller. We are going westbound on Blesser, hoping he turns."

Several minutes passed with three FBI units attempting to regain sight of the Ford. Then, "I got him eastbound on Blesser," hollered Ali, the adrenaline starting to kick in. We will stay with him and try to get a DPD unit to stop him. One and Two converge to this area."

While this was going on, Harley was on the phone to the emergency call center.

"This is 911, what is your emergency?"

"Listen carefully. This is FBI Agent Harley Jennings. We are following a black Ford sedan eastbound, Mississippi license plate Alpha, Echo, Lima, 8151, now northbound Kingsley approaching Warren. We need a DPD unit to stop a possible DUI suspect who is driving erratically and could hurt someone."

"Okay, stand by. All units, FBI is requesting assistance on a black Ford sedan, Mississippi license Alpha, Echo,

Lima, 8151, northbound Kingsley approaching Warren, possible DUI. What kind of car are you in, Agent?"

"It's a late-model silver Chevy; I don't have the plate," said Ali. Suspect is now now eastbound on Warren."

Spotting a DPD-marked police unit hauling ass towards them, Harley flashed his brights. Screeching the tires, the police SUV slowed down to make the turn and fell behind the black Ford. As the unit positioned itself and activated its emergency lights, the suspect made a right turn on Freda Street, speeding into the Huron Apartments complex, and jumped out. He wasn't fast enough, as both officers were on him immediately: "Stop, police!" The suspect turned towards the two officers as if deciding if it would be worth a try to run. "Put your hands on the car's hood; do it now," yelled the driver officer, the more senior of the two.

While this was happening, Harley pulled behind the police car, waiting for an opportunity to speak to one of the officers. Just then, a second DPD unit pulled alongside them. Seeing his officers had the suspect under control, the sergeant stepped over to Harley, who ID'd himself.

"So, what do you need, Agent?"

"Thanks, Sarge. We are working a case on this man and followed him from a bar when he took off. He was driving like he was DUI. If your officers could give him a field sobriety test and take him to the station, we could go through his car before it is impounded. I should also mention that this case has national security implications."

As the police supervisor checked his two officers' progress, he said, "No problem, sir. I can do it. Let's see how they handle it first."

"Please call me Harley."

“Yes, sir, Harley.”

After completing the FST on their own accord, the officers handcuffed the suspect and put him in the back of their police car. With the suspect secured, the driver officer approached his sergeant, who asked, "What do you have, John?"

"Sarge, this guy smells of alcohol, so we gave him the FST, which he failed. We want to take him to the station and give him a breathalyzer."

"Okay, sounds good. I will impound the car for you unless the guy lives here."

“No, he says he's from Mississippi, just visiting some friends."

"Was he cooperative?" asked Harley.

John looked at his supervisor to see if he should be talking to this guy in civilian clothes.

"It's okay; these guys are both FBI, working a case on your subject."

Looking at Harley, "Yes, sir, very cooperative. He even called us 'sir' and did everything we told him to do."

"Did he volunteer any information about what he was doing?" asked Harley.

"No, sir, just answered our questions—the usual stuff. Though at one point, he did ask who you were."

"What did you tell him, officer?" asked Harley.

"I said I didn't know, perhaps some concerned citizens. One more thing, sir. This guy seems like he's ex-military; it's just how he handles himself, not your usual flake."

"Thank you, John. We appreciate your observations; that helps us a lot."

"Okay, John, take our boy to the station and let me know what he blows."

"Okay, Sarge, will do."

After the police unit departed, Harley and Ali searched the Ford. The interior was spotless, as was the trunk. The only thing they found was a receipt from Super Greenland Market on West Warren under the front seat. The two agents hoped this might help lead them to his residence, as neither believed he was passing through. Both men agreed; they were definitely on to something.

Chapter 19

Dearborn Police Department

Dearborn, Michigan

At the police station, Ahmad only blew a .03, and it was decided to kick him loose so the FBI could put a new tail on him. Unit Two was sitting near the station, so it followed the Uber carrying Ahmad to a Circle 8 motel on Michigan Avenue. As he walked into the lobby, the terrorist didn't even glance over his shoulder; he knew he was being followed.

Picking a room near the rear of the lot, Ahmad entered, pausing long enough to make sure whoever was following him saw it was him. He guessed they were Dearborn PD detectives or perhaps even the FBI. When he entered, he turned on the light by the front window. He took off his bulky blue sweater, revealing his black pullover. After waiting for fifteen minutes, he turned off the light. Ahmad waited another ten minutes to ensure no one came sniffing around his room, then climbed out a back window.

Taking a route where he was sure his pursuers could not see him, Ahmad walked two blocks to a 7-Eleven and called Umair, telling him briefly what had happened. Borrowing a car from one of his associates, Umair picked up Ahmad, and they drove to his house.

As Umair was parking the car in the driveway, Ahmad invited him inside for a beer despite how late it was getting. "Sure," said Umair, shutting off the engine. After sitting down in the small living room, Umair asked, "So, what's up with the law following you?"

"That's a good question, and another would be 'Why'? For the 'who,' I can only believe it's the cops from DPD who were following you and found me. I suppose it could be the FBI, but that would be a stretch as there is no way I should have come up on their radar. I have made sure to cover all my tracks. The 'why' has to be they think I'm joining your gang and want more information, so they do a bogus stop and take me in to gather it. They don't know I live here, and I want to keep it that way. Anyway, I appreciate you giving me a ride."

"Sure, no problem."

Taking a sip of his beer, Ahmad said, "Since they know my car now, I'm going to leave it in impound and buy some cheap ride to get me by. I'll just use my Mississippi ID. Anyway, did you get a chance to look at the videos I sent you?"

"Sure did," said Umair. "I have always been proud of my heritage, but watching those videos brought it home. I don't remember the July War, as I was only six or something, but I remember hiding in the basement of our building when Israeli jets were bombing our city. Afterward, I recall playing in a bombed-out building. I sure didn't know the Israelis slaughtered over a thousand of our countrymen. But that one video made it clear how the Americans have done whatever they can to support Israel at our expense."

"It pisses me off," said Ahmad, "how our country is constantly being attacked, and the US is behind most of it, through the Israelis. I can only tell you things will change soon. I know."

"What do you mean?" asked Umair.

"I can't say right now, but there may come a time when I need your help, with Allah's blessing, to strike back."

"I hear you, brother. I stand ready."

Chapter 20

Hamtramck, Michigan

As she made her father's bed, Lieutenant Commander Sarah "Danger" Freeman was thinking about what she missed most about the Navy. It must be the adrenaline rush of flying off a carrier, she thought. From zero to one-sixty in just seconds. Hard to beat that. But she had to admit, there was also an ache in her heart for her conceited F-35 fighter pilot, Jessie Hampton. Theirs had been an on-again, off-again relationship ever since the two met while being rescued from the South China Sea during the war with China. That was five years ago. But as hard as the two lovers tried to keep it together, the Navy and their flying careers got in the way.

Well, she thought, one more try. Jessie would be arriving soon, on leave, and they both had agreed it was time to make this work or move on—which she sure didn't want to happen.

Sarah was on leave of sorts herself. Her father was very sick, and none of his doctors could pinpoint what was slowly robbing him of his life. She was in week seven of her allotted twenty-six weeks of unpaid leave to care for him. She was the only one left in his life and she loved him so—but it was challenging. With non-stop doctor appointments, trips to the drug store, and housekeeping, Sarah was missing her time in the cockpit of her E-2 Hawkeye, having been on her third tour aboard the USS *Reagan*.

"Sarah, where's the coffee?"

"Dad, I'll be right there and help you."

"I don't need any help," her father yelled back, even though they were just two rooms apart. Sarah hustled into the kitchen, where her father scanned the cupboards like he had lost his best friend inside one of them.

"Dad, don't you remember I bought you a Keurig coffee maker? Here, let me show you," she said. After sitting him down at the kitchen table, she went through the motions—again. Poor thing, he was becoming more forgetful.

With two fresh cups of brew, their Sunday morning was off and running. Sarah loved her coffee steaming hot and took a big gulp, feeling the warmth all the way down. "So, Dad, Jessie will be arriving Tuesday and—"

Interrupting his daughter, "Who's Jessie?" he said matter-of-factly.

"He's my boyfriend—of sorts. You met him a couple of years ago at my promotion ceremonies. You said he seems like a nice guy but walks like he owns the world."

"Oh yeah, I remember now. Why is he coming here? We sure as hell don't have much room."

"He's staying in my room—and don't go there, Daddy."

Not listening: "Your Mom and I weren't in the same bed until our wedding night." With that, Sarah saw him quickly glaze over as he went back fifty-some years. Good for him, she thought; at least he was in a happy place for a few seconds. "Okay, Dad, finish your coffee so we can take our morning walk to the park."

"What for? We were just there."

"I know, but you like to watch the kids play while you sit on your favorite bench." Her Dad nodded. With that, the decorated Naval flight aviator started her day by counting the hours until Jessie was by her side—telling her more of his war stories.

Chapter 21

Dearborn, Michigan

Ahmad was not one to sit idly around his house, especially with such a vital mission brewing. With the police on his ass, it was time to act. It had to start with Samir. Ahmad called him on his secure phone.

Samir answered on the first ring. "Assalamu alaikum."

"Alaikum salaam," replied Samir.

"I wanted to tell you about an encounter with the police."

"The police?" exclaimed Samir.

After going over the details of meeting with Umair and being arrested and taken to the police station, Ahmad said, "They didn't book me, but they did take my fingerprints before they let me go. So now they know who I am, but that's about it. They will probably watch me, so we should ensure we're never seen together. I can handle the police."

"But why would they be following you?"

"I would guess because the bar is known to the police as a gang hangout, and since I was a stranger visiting, they decided to follow me and then take me to jail to get my prints and personal information."

After thinking for a moment, Samir said, "I sure don't like that the police are aware of you, but since they have nothing else, we should be good. I think you must make every effort to ensure you are not being followed at all times." Moving on, he asked, "How's it going with Umair? Are you winning him over to our cause?"

"Most definitely," said Ahmad. "He is a very devoted Lebanese man who just needed to be reminded of where his roots are. He's to the point where he would do anything I asked of him. But I must say, I can't figure out why we need him."

"I understand your question, but we will discuss that further at the appropriate time." Then, a pause. Ahmad could tell by his voice something more was coming, and it did. "There are two things we need to discuss as we proceed." Ahmad could feel the adrenaline in his body elevate as he waited for Samir to continue. "We need you to go to Philadelphia to reconnoiter the area and prepare for your mission. You are to go to the Walmart on the northeast corner of the parking lot, the one by your house, and I will have Mustafa meet you there and hand over some cash and a car for you to drive to Philadelphia. You will travel alone. We want to keep this mission on a need-to-know basis only. The fewer people involved in the planning stage, the better.

Lodging is up to you, but pay cash for everything, including gas. Do not use any of your credit cards—ever.”

Feeling exhilarated that things were progressing, Ahmad tried to control his emotions, but his voice skipped an octave when he said, "Yes, Samir, I understand."

"Second, I now want to tell you what weapon you will use for the attack so that you can plan accordingly. I was told you fired scores of rounds in your training and are very proficient with—."

Ahmad couldn't hold back, "The M72!"

"Ahmad, please let me finish. Yes, it will be an M72 armed with the Anti-Structure Munition."

Excited, Ahmad interjected, "Yes, Samir, I used that particular round many times on concrete structures—the amount of destruction it delivers is incredible."

"All right, prepare for your trip and pack light; you won't be there long. Take only a backpack, no suitcase. May Allah be with you in everything you do."

Chapter 22

Detroit Metropolitan Wayne County Airport
Detroit, Michigan

Sarah felt a little lightheaded as she watched the faces rush by her while she waited at the exit gate at Detroit Metro. She was interested in just one face, Jessie Hampton's—her boyfriend, if you can use that term for someone her age. The twitter in her heart came from her love for the guy versus their constant conflict to make this 'thing' work. Both loved to fly for the Navy and since they were on different carriers, this separation didn't help the on-and-off love affair. But they both agreed it was now or never; it was time to go all in—or fold for good.

Suddenly, someone grabbed her from behind. She couldn't help but let a little scream slip out. As she turned around, there he was, the sneaky bastard, with a huge shit-eating grin on his face like he had just scored another win in a dogfight. After she almost peed her pants, she jumped up on him, wrapping her arms around his neck. Jessie held her tight, twirling her around in slow motion. It was a moment neither would ever forget. Just for that moment, the entire world stopped, and it was only the two of them, slowly whirling in a circle together and in love.

"My gosh," said Jessie, "I can't believe how much I missed you," breaking off his words to give Sarah a passionate kiss.

Sarah responded softly, "Jessie, we have to make this work—it's too good."

Letting her land softly, like catching the third wire on the *Ford*, Jessie was lost in Sarah's deep green eyes and her radiant smile. Throwing on his backpack, which had a permanently embossed "Go Navy beat Army" stamp, they were off to her dad's house in Hamtramck, hand in hand.

Once at the house, Jessie couldn't believe how much Sarah's dad had deteriorated since he'd last seen him. As they shook hands, it felt like he had no grip; it was more like a sponge than the firm grip he was used to. Jessie whispered to Sarah in her room, where he committed to doing whatever he could to help. Sarah thanked him by giving him a gentle hug and thought about how they were off to a positive start.

Chapter 23

Joint Terrorism Task Force, JTTF

FBI Field Office, Detroit, Michigan

As the lead agents in anything to do with terrorism, Harley Jennings and Ali Mohsen sat in the front of the room, which served as the briefing location for the meeting. Present for the monthly conference of the JTTF were representatives from several agencies who all shared one common link: their expertise with terrorism. Included were representatives from the Michigan Department of Corrections, Michigan State Police, Sheriffs' Association, US Department of Homeland Security, Michigan State University Police Department, and several local police agencies. As one unified team of experts, each conference built awareness, the sharing of criminal intelligence, and, most importantly, working relationships. Fifty-five other FBI field offices were accomplishing the same goal. Together, their joint effort improved the ability to detect and prevent acts of terrorism and other crimes, keeping the nation safer through their actions.

As the meeting was about to start, the two agents sitting at the front of the room were not surprised to see the SAC, John Williamson, stroll into the room.

"Just in time, I see," he said, throwing it out to the room. "We have a special guest today, and I wanted to introduce her." Looking over at the woman sitting in the front row, he continued, "It's my pleasure to introduce Norma Silverston from Cybersecurity and Infrastructure Security Agency, also known as CISA. She is a retired Army colonel who is the second-in-command of the agency's energy sector and has a heads-up warning for us. Ms. Silverston."

Walking to the front of the room and behind a podium with a large FBI plaque prominently displayed, the forty-something woman looked nothing like your typical bureaucrat or Army brass but like a pleasant-looking, well-dressed lady of the world.

"Thank you, Agent Williamson." She wasted no time on her message. "Ladies and gentlemen, if we in law enforcement don't do our job of protecting the electrical infrastructure of this nation, we all could be living in the dark, fighting to maintain anything resembling life as we know it. Imagine if you would, doctors watching as their patients die because the ventilators don't work. There would be thousands trapped in elevators; electrical appliances wouldn't work; ATMs would be down, banks and businesses would shut down; there would be no gas or electricity for your car, and eventually, no food in your favorite grocery store. Drinking water would become a premium—forget flushing your toilet. Martial law would be implemented, but there would not be enough personnel to enforce it. The military would be mostly helpless, riots would begin, and people would fight over food to eat and water to drink. Only 10 percent of the American population would survive if the shutdown lasted a year. It sounds like that could never happen. Well, I suggest you think again."

As she eyed the room, she saw she had everyone's attention; even the SAC was still in the doorway. "Last year, there were over 150 reported attacks on power stations, which is an all-time high. The weapon of choice in most instances was a high-powered rifle. Fortunately for the good guys, most criminals are dumb and just shoot up the place. But be warned; it would only take a few educated terrorists to bring about what I just described. Case in point: In Washington County near San Francisco last year, a small group of saboteurs attacked several power stations, causing $20 million in damages and shutting down power to 75,000 people for days. These saboteurs were quite sophisticated in concentrating their efforts to shut down one portion of the country. Unfortunately, we have yet to make any arrests.

"I understand we have a monumental task. Protecting the 11,925 electric power plants, the 79,000 transmission substations, and the 160,000 miles of high-voltage power lines makes it a particularly soft target for determined attackers. Unfortunately, it's vulnerable because of how it was constructed. Consequently, if one part of it can be destroyed or impaired, it can quickly impact other larger parts. Knock one domino down and watch out as the rest fall." Several hands went up as she stopped to take a sip of water.

"Let me finish my point, and then I can answer your questions. With most power stations only protected by your typical chain-link fence and often isolated, it doesn't take a sophisticated criminal to succeed. What concerns my colleagues and me is that the bad guys are quickly learning that they need to concentrate their fire on the large transformers and circuit breakers. Today, much of this targeted information has found its way to the web.

"Even though we in the law enforcement community are aware of the threats to our electrical grid, and steps have been taken to upgrade security, we acknowledge that the attacks will continue. A relentless enemy with knowledge gained from the web knows what to shoot and how to cripple the power station's key components, after which they fade to the underground to strike again. But for us, as terrorist experts, meeting and discussing these threats is the first step in using sound intelligence to track these bastards down and prevent these attacks that are on the increase. And I have not even discussed the cyber threat by foreign countries; that is another subject for another time. Questions?"

After answering questions, Ms. Silverston left the room, and Ali took the floor. "I wanted to share some intel Harley, and I have been gathering that has its roots with the Warren Bros street gang from Dearborn. I see John from the DPD gang unit in the room, so please add what you know after my brief.

"We became aware through intelligence that a possible Hezbollah terrorist was using the Muslim Center of Michigan as a staging area, for what we are not sure. During a stakeout, we saw Umair Sabar, the leader of the Bros, meet with this possible terrorist and disappear inside. I quickly followed them and tracked them down to the library, where I was met by a huge man we call the giant. He is, without question, a professional Hezbollah soldier who fills every check box for his job. Trying to pass himself off as one of the mosque aides, he kicked me out of the library, but not before I saw the two men hiding in the back of the stacks."

Judging from the looks on everyone's faces, the terrorist specialists were interested to see where this was going. Ali didn't hold back. "Putting their hangout, Tip a Few bar, under surveillance, Harley and I decided to roll the dice and surveil the place from inside. Well, needless to say, that sure as hell didn't work, as I'm sure most of you heard. Before we were hauled off to jail"—which had the room cutting up with laughter—"I encountered another Lebanese man, who appeared to be American. Once again, he had all the mannerisms of a professional Hezbollah operative, something I noticed when he hit me in the face with a right." That got them all laughing again.

"Later, in another surveillance operation, we saw this same man drive up to the bar and enter. When he left, we had three units tailing him. He got wise to this immediately and tried to give us the slip. We called DPD, and they picked him up and took him to jail, where we got his ID. His name is Ahmad Nadar, with his last known residence in Mississippi. He's been arrested twice for fighting, with no convictions. We have yet to establish where he lives. I am passing out some photos of Nadar so you can keep an eye open for him. With what appears to be three Hezbollah terrorists in town, I'm sure you, like me, don't believe in coincidences. John, what can you share about Sabar?"

"Well, Ali, I can't add anything to your assessment. Sabar has always been a gangbanger who specializes in dealing drugs. I have not uncovered any other criminal activity and didn't know he was hanging with a known terrorist. We have a CI, and I will drill him again to see if he knows anything. I'll keep you and the group informed—because it sure looks like something is up, and I don't like it." No one in the room did.

Chapter 24

Independence Hall

Philadelphia, Pennsylvania

Ahmad Nadar looked and acted like the hundreds of other visitors coming to Philadelphia's Historic District, with its centerpiece, Independence Hall. He headed for his first stop, the Independence Visitor Center, just down the grassy parkland from his target. Ahmad wore nondescript clothes he had bought at Walmart consisting of blue jeans and a dark plaid shirt; he didn’t want to stand out to security. His intent as a Hezbollah soldier was never to earn a second look. His mission was to scout the area for his planned destruction of Independence Hall and everything it represented in America.

Ahmad stood at the 42-foot interactive touchscreen digital wall inside the visitor's center to get a sense of the area's layout. He then watched an eight-minute film in the open-walled theater. When he was done, he purchased his tickets for the Hall, bought some lunch, and sat outside, which allowed him a great view of Independence Hall, which seemed dwarfed by two skyscrapers behind it. The terrorist couldn't help but picture what the view would be like after he sent two M72 Anti-Structure Munition missiles through the front door. He had to smile at the vision.

Finishing his lunch and daydream, Ahmad followed the suggested route from his pamphlet and headed down Market Street to the Liberty Bell Center to view the "iconic symbol of freedom" that had a crack in it. He passed through the security screening line to enter, and a red light went off. Ahmad had forgotten to take his cell phone out of his pocket. With that removed, he got waved through, but in his peripheral vision he noticed a third uniformed security guard who seemed much more attentive than the two guards at the metal detector. It appeared to Ahmad this was no ordinary rent-a-cop. He looked like he had been around the block a few times. Ahmad made a mental note to watch for this man.

Playing the part of a tourist, Ahmad took a few pictures and walked a short distance until he stood directly in front of his target. He moved among the other tourists, stopping at places he thought essential, and faked taking a selfie to get pictures of the structure and possible targeting points. Moving to just the right spot, Ahmad took some close-ups using the zoom function on his phone's camera. Satisfied he had what he needed, he followed the other tourists to the rear of the building to begin the tour.

There was another security screening area at the rear of the building, and he passed through it quickly while keeping an eye open for the third guard. Ahmad didn't see him, but he had a gut feeling he was being watched. Whatever, he was just another tourist snapping pictures at random—or so it appeared.

Soon, it was his turn to enter the Hall. A park ranger led his group of around fifty inside. But Ahmad's concentration was not on what the ranger was spewing off but on the windows and their relationship to what was in the interior. He already knew, but the ranger confirmed that the building was made of solid red brick covered with white marble and granite, with walls up to twenty-two feet thick at the bottom. He noted that it was much better to go through the windows than the thick walls. These were essential calculations for choosing the proper rounds for his M72 and where to place them.

In the Assembly Room, the group was told it was one of the most historic rooms in the United States as it was here that the Continental Congress declared independence in 1776. Twenty-one years later, the US Constitution was debated and signed. What a perfect target, he thought to himself. Praise be to Allah for taking him on this journey.

Ahmad noted the long gallery on the second floor with about twenty feet of hallway between the windows and the interior wall. More details to consider.

After the twenty-minute tour, Ahmad walked the surrounding area looking for possible launch points. He knew from his training that the effective range was 350 to 1000 meters. Ahmad documented this with pictures he took from different angles and locations. As he walked from the area, he thanked Allah again for blessing him with this mission and prayed for his success, which he thought was looking very probable.

Chapter 25

Independence Hall

Philadelphia, Pennsylvania

Walking the grounds of Independence Hall was an assignment Kordell Jackson took seriously—but then, he took everything seriously. One of Kordell's strong points in life had always been his ability to see things not as they appeared, but with a discerning mind that looked beyond that. On the job, his observation arrests had been off the charts. This meant he made arrests not from receiving a radio call, but seeing something that just didn't fit the circumstances. Kordell would then use his investigative and intuitive genius to assemble the criminal puzzle and make an arrest. It's a trait not unlike common sense in life; either you have it, or you don't. He had it in spades.

As a black child growing up on the other side of the tracks, Kordell had to fight for everything, starting with his lunch money. Gangs didn't care much for a kid who refused to join them. Many called him an "Uncle Tom." But through it all, he remained strong to the ideals his parents instilled in him from the time he took his first steps. Have a positive attitude, be of service to others, have a strong character, hang with the right people, discover your life's purpose, and go for it.

It's a crazy world with crazy people, and Kordell was at the Hall to ensure the treasured symbol of his country's freedom would never suffer any setbacks. On the streets of Philadelphia, he'd had the respect of the citizens, but not so much here—that was an adjustment. He wasn't sure why this was the case, perhaps because of his color and his occupation as a security guard, which didn't bring much acclaim. So, Kordell adjusted as he always had done; he devoted himself to his work.

Having decided to get out of the confines of the Hall and into some fresh air, Kordell was scrutinizing the area around the Liberty Bell when he heard the beep from the security screening area, meaning someone had metal on their person. Even though the sensitivity was set relatively high, the device still would sound off on larger metal objects. He noticed a young man stop and go back through after depositing his phone in a container. As the young man did so, he glanced over at Kordell, and the two locked eyes. Instantly, Kordell's cop instinct set off warning bells. It was the look and demeanor that told the former street cop this was not your average twenty-something checking out the bell. Something about this man made him stand out—

something that any streetwise cop does not turn his back on. It warranted a second look. As the man took pictures of the bell, Kordell caught him sneaking another glance in his direction. Kordell put on a disinterested look and headed back toward the Hall. He had an idea.

Concealed on the second floor of Independence Hall is a security area with a bank of monitors being fed signals from around the entire complex, with both interior and exterior views. A security guard can sit in there most of the day and monitor activity, or, as Kordell preferred, be among the guests to be seen as a deterrent to crime or mischief.

Kordell felt that if his senses were correct, the man would be watching his six to see if anyone was following him. Kordell didn't want to spook the man, but he wanted to confirm or eliminate him from his suspicions.

Knowing the route most individuals take, Kordell monitored the camera feed aimed at the grassy expanse in front of the Hall. With the ability to zoom in on his camera's focal point, it only took seconds to spot the man moving around the area, taking selfies and photos of the Hall. Having watched thousands of people take pictures over the past year, Kordell knew the norm. This was not it. The man was taking lots of photos. If he had a professional rig, that would be one thing, but with a cell phone, it was excessive compared to other visitors. Kordell marked down the current time so he could group the recorded videos together if needed.

The suspect, as Kordell always thought of anyone he looked at twice, walked to the back of the building, taking pictures as he did so. As the man went through security, his neck was on a swivel, checking out the area around him, evidently looking for Kordell. Noted.

As Swivel Head was on the tour, Kordell noticed that he seemed interested in the window placement and what was behind them. This was especially true on the second floor, where he took several pictures of the hallway and the windows.

After the tour, Swivel Head returned to the grassy parkland where he had been earlier. This time, he was taking pictures of the entire area. From there, he faded from sight beyond the Visitors Center. Kordell felt that Swivel Head needed a follow-up. After downloading some footage, he ran it by his boss, Sam Wiggins.

After viewing the video footage, Sam agreed this man needed further investigation. He knew the PPD department's liaison with JTTF and got the footage over to him. They ran the suspect's image through the FBI's facial recognition software and immediately got a hit. According to FBI records, Swivel Head's name was Ahmad Nadar, and he recently became a person of interest in an ongoing investigation by the Detroit office of the FBI. The information was immediately relayed to their Counter Terrorism Department. Nadar quickly passed from being a person of interest to having an FBI spotlight on him—something he wouldn't see.

Chapter 26

FBI Field Office

Detroit, Michigan

As meetings go, this one was set up quickly. Present in the conference room were all the members from the Counterterrorism Division and his boss, John Williamson, who opened the meeting. "Okay folks, as you all heard, it appears we have some serious shit going on with our friend, Ahmad Nadar. I want us to put our heads together this morning and determine what we have and how best to handle it. Harley and Ali have the lead on this. Guys."

"Thanks, SAC," said Harley. "To ensure we are all on the same page, here is what we have so far on Nadar. He is an American citizen of Lebanese descent who grew up in Mississippi. From what we have determined, he had a troubled childhood that continued through high school. The man would just as soon fight you as to look at you, and he was good at it. Once, he was kicked out of high school for breaking the nose of some kid. Soon after, Nadar switched to traditional Lebanese clothing and distanced himself from being identified as an American.

"He worked odd jobs, and we don't hear from him again until his travel documents reveal that when he was twenty-two, he flew to Athens. Here we lose him; he doesn't appear on the radar again until his return flight from Turkey to Mississippi months later."

At this point, Ali interjected. "Not wanting to leave his tracks behind, it appears that Nadar used ground transportation to get to and from Lebanon, where we feel he went to join Hezbollah and obtain terrorist training. The timing seems right, and we feel confident he was not on some personal getaway. After a few months, Nadar flew back to Mississippi and soon after was in Dearborn, where he tried to knock me out at a Lebanese gang bar. We are faced with the question of why he is here. We can only speculate. One is that we expect he is soliciting the help of the Warren Bros drug-dealing street gang for reasons we know nothing about."

As they had rehearsed, Harley came back into the presentation for the Philly segment. "But this entire investigation transformed when Nadar showed up in Philadelphia and happened to arouse the suspicions of a seasoned Philadelphia Street cop who now works private security at Independence Hall. We have closely examined the video he supplied, and it is clear that Nadar has more than a passing interest in the Hall. He was taking pictures as part of what appears to be an intelligence-gathering mission for something we feel is a prelude to a possible attack. Once again, we are not sure, but nothing can be ruled out, including a concentrated terrorist attack on our nation's symbol of freedom—Independence Hall—an ideal target for Hezbollah and its propaganda machine. A radicalized American citizen who can move freely in our country is a potential threat to everyone."

From one of the agents: "Do we have enough to pick him up?"

Harley answered, "We have discussed this with several others, and no, not enough for detention. Plus, we must locate him again. We have two cameras placed around Tip a Few, so if he shows up, we will be alerted and can go from there. We will also be keeping an eye on Sabar and his gang."

The SAC added, "I have directed our team to inform the National Counterterrorism Center of the specifics of our case and to flag any information that might come in from other agencies regarding Nadar or any other players from this area."

Another agent added, "If this man received training in Lebanon or Iran, well, judging from his time there, I would suggest we face a significant threat. We all know of the sophistication of their terrorist training, including all sorts of weapons training that Nadar could use for an attack anywhere in the US. And one more thing, we all know he is probably not acting alone—there will be others."

"I agree," added Harley. We need to work our CIs and put our ears to the ground to gather street intelligence on what is going on out there. People know, and people talk. Be selective with your questions; we don't want to spook the man. We want to find him and find out what he's up to." The entire room nodded in agreement—they all agreed, something was up.

Chapter 27

10-Ring Firing Range
Dearborn, Michigan

Pulling up to the 10-Ring Firing Range, Sarah and Jessie were still arguing about why Sarah should be driving, even though it was her dad's car. "Look, Mr. Fighter Pilot, just because you fly F-35s doesn't mean you should be driving my dad's Porsche."

"I'm sorry, Sarah. It does. I'm made to go fast. My instincts and reaction time are split-seconds in the air and sure as hell doesn't change on the ground."

Sarah thought, well if you're so damn good, how'd you manage to get shot down during the Chinese war? But she knew where that would lead. Instead: "Bullshit, Jessie! If you recall, a Chinese J-20 nearly took me out during the war, and through my piloting skills, I saved my ass and the crew. I received a nice commendation for that."

As they got out of the car, Jessie asked, "Whatever. Remind me again why we are coming here?"

"Because," said Sarah with conviction, "just because you can fire missiles and machine guns from your fighter jet doesn't mean you can protect yourself down here on Earth."

Grabbing two cases from the front trunk, she added, "I think it's essential for home defense and something you should be proficient with. Besides, it's fun. My dad taught me how to shoot when I was old enough to hold a BB gun, shooting balloons gliding across the pond at our summer cabin."

As they entered the business, they met a tattooed, bearded guy who looked like a survivalist who had just endured the first end-of-the-world gig. It surprised them how friendly he was.

"Hi guys, how may I help you?" he said with an ear-to-ear smile. It looks like you have some shooting in mind. Whatcha you carrying in their cases?"

Sarah shot him back a huge smile. "How about one Sig Sauer M17 and one Colt M1911A1," she said proudly.

"I thought so; you two both look like military folk and judging from your sidearms of choice, I'd say I'm right."

"You nailed it," said Jessie, already liking this dude. He reminded him of some of the guys he flew with, minus the long beard.

"I'm retired Army and did my share of time in Iraq and Afghanistan. Anyway, you came to the right place cause the boss man gives active military ten percent off on the range and ammo—not bad, eh?"

"Fuckin' A," said Jessie, getting a look from Sarah, who was surprised by his sudden interest and energy.

"Okay, I have you on lane four. It's busy, so expect a lot of shooting." Both Sarah and Jessie could hear someone firing a high-powered rifle, a sound that separated itself from the other gunshots. They immediately put on ear protection and headed for their assigned lane.

As they arrived, they noticed three younger men who appeared to be of Middle Eastern descent next to them in lane five. One of the men was holding a rifle. The men were so intent on what they were doing that they didn't even look up as Sarah and Jessie pulled their weapons from their cases. The group seemed to be arguing about what rounds the rifle takes.

Sarah had Jessie pose for her, and as she took the picture, the man with the rifle walked into the background, so she took another one. "Come on, Sarah, this isn't a photo shoot. Let's go so I can show you who rules the range."

"Sure, Jessie, but do you even know—"

Just then, the man with an assault-looking rifle fired several rounds in rapid succession. Whatever he was using, it was one powerful weapon. Sarah could feel the concussion from the rifle even several feet away.

As the two Navy pilots fine-tuned their marksmanship, Sarah couldn't help but overhear some of the conversations between the three men. Most of what she heard had to do with rounds that would penetrate metal, which she thought was strange. Why would they want bullets that would fire through metal? Oh well, she thought, none of her business.

After Sarah outshot Jessie and made sure he acknowledged it, they packed their gear and headed out. As they got into the Porsche, with Sarah behind the wheel, they saw the three men exit the range. They watched as one got into a raised red Dodge Ram with oversized off-road tires. Sarah couldn't tell you why, but she made a mental note of the license plate; she was weird that way.

Chapter 28

Islamic Revolutionary Guard Corps, IRGC

19th Fajr Brigade, undisclosed location in Syria

Seven thousand miles away from Dearborn, events were transpiring, set in motion by the Supreme Leader to fulfill his prophecy of putting his nation in the news, making it clear he was the all-encompassing leader. Hezbollah would be his proxy. His plan was to strike fear in the world by using well-chosen terrorist attacks. He also understood that for Hezbollah to be feared, fear must be placed in the hearts of the infidels. Done correctly, the eyes of the world would be focused on Syria and not their target in the United States.

Standing over a muddy field with a commanding view was Colonel Masoud Shahryar, lead instructor of the IRGC. "Dammit, Sergeant," he yelled, "tell your men to keep the machine gun fire going, no let-up." No sooner had the words left his lips than the fire intensified.

On the flanks, explosives continued to go off, throwing dirt in the air and providing limited visibility for the soldiers. It was nearly impossible to hear or give commands. Crawling under long strands of barbed wire just inches from their backs and, for some, their chest, were fifty of Iran's most elite men, the Quds, Iran's special forces. Low crawling underneath the wire with bullets passing just inches above them, they understood that if you spooked and started to get up or even stretch above the wire, you were a dead man.

One of the dirty faces crawling along with his Iranian-made Fateh rifle straddled between his outstretched arms was Captain Amir Asgari. He could have easily been standing on the sidelines supervising his men, but Asgari was not that person; he led by example. Asgari grew up in the poorest provinces of Iran: Sistan and Baluchestan. Always seemingly without food or money, he learned to survive as a thief. As a teenager, he led raiding parties into neighboring Pakistan to steal from people who had little more than he did. When he was seventeen, he met an Iranian Army soldier who was visiting his village. Hearing the man's stories, Asgari decided this was the life for him. Now, leading as usual, with bullets flying just above his head, he was in paradise—his paradise.

A siren sounded as his squad of men reached the end of the large field. Immediately, the bombs and machine gun fire ceased. Asgari jumped up, brushed himself off, and gathered his men in the shade of a lone tree. There was excited chatter as men exchanged stories about the exercise.

"Shut up," yelled the most senior of all the troops, Chief Warrant Officer Arash Hashem, a burly five-foot, ten-inch chiseled stud who had seen more action than most of his men combined. "You sound like a bunch of school kids at recess." Within a millisecond, it was so quiet that the men could hear a lone fly buzzing around their sweaty, dirty bodies.

"Okay, I get it," said Captain Asgari. "You are probably wondering why you were put through this drill again since most of you have done it countless times in the past. I'll tell you why: Because I thought it was time you got shot at again. It's been a while. But that's going to change right now. After we finish at the range, I want you to prepare for a mission we don't often get—to bring the fight to the infidels from America right here in Syria." Taking his cover off to wipe sweat from his forehead and to let his words sink in, Asgari continued. "We have intel that the US is building up their base at Al-Tanf Garrison to give them a stronger foothold in that part of Syria. Our Supreme Leader has told me personally this is not going to happen. It's time we put headlines in the world press to demonstrate that Americans have no right to be in Syria or any part of the Middle East. We will deliver that message loud and clear."

Chapter 29

Near Al-Tanf Garrison

Southeastern Syria

As the sun rose over the arid landscape of southeastern Syria, a twelve-man American patrol made their way off-road, cautiously, to avoid any possible IEDs. It was dusty and bumpy, but they had the right vehicle to accomplish their task. Driving along in an M-ATV with its sixteen-inch ground clearance, passing over ruts like they weren't there, the soldiers were on a strategic reconnaissance mission from the elite Operational Detachment Alpha, 5th Special Forces Group—the Green Berets. They were heads-up searching for IRGC gun runners. The terrorist group was known to be smuggling guns into Iran through the cover of war-ravaged Syria using their east-west land corridor stretching from Syria to Iran to Lebanon. But habitually, the terrorists always made a wide arch around the US base of Al-Tanf. The twelve specially trained soldiers knew this and were making the same arc, hoping they would spot the enemy before their location was given away by the vehicle-induced dust clouds that could rise hundreds of feet into the air.

Captain Roger Ashburger was sitting on a blast seat on the commander's side of the fully armored M-ATV, stroking his long dirty beard, contemplating what route the enemy might take through this shit hole of a country. He tried his best to block out the chatter from the other four soldiers in the vehicle. Two M1288 GMV Special Forces tactical vehicles modified as Flyer 72s followed in his dust.

"Sherwood," said Ashburger, "let's take that hill just ahead and have a look-see."

"Got it, sir."

"Stargazer to Moonshadow One and Two, stand by at the base of this hill. We are going to glass the area from up top."

It wasn't much of a hill, by Ashburger's terms, because he grew up in the Rocky Mountains of Colorado. But out here in the desert, you take what you can get.

Stopping short of the top, Ashburger and his comms specialist, Sergeant Andy Boykin, dismounted, making sure not to silhouette themselves against the skyline. They pulled out their M22 binoculars and began scanning the area. They were looking for telltale signs like a dust trail, metal reflections, anything. It didn't take long.

"Target, your 10," exclaimed Ashburger.

"Got it. Looks like three pickups heading west, 1800 meters out. All have covered cargo. Estimated speed, 30 kilometers per hour."

"Get on the line and see if we have eyes on this area," said Ashburger. "I want to get ahead of them and set up an ambush."

Ali Al Salem Air Base

Kuwait

Scanning the vast expanse of the Syrian Desert through the video cameras aboard his MQ-9 Reaper, Captain Frank Rodgers and his sensor operator Tech Sergeant Tim Withers had just received information from a Special Forces team of possible enemy activity. Traveling at 260 knots, the Reaper drone was closing the distance to the last reported sighting of three civilian pickup trucks heading west.

There is one absolute rule in the desert: Travel by day, and your dust trail might give you away should anyone be looking. Today, they were.

Withers didn't have to say it while adjusting the electro-optical and infrared sensors; Rodgers saw it on the large color monitor hanging in front of him. Through the dust, both operators saw the heat signature of three trucks traveling close together. With a smooth motion of his control stick, the veteran drone operator silently guided the drone to an ideal altitude of 15,000 feet, closing on his targets. While Rodgers was maneuvering the aircraft into position, Withers fine-tuned the sensors to get eyes on and better understand what they had.

As both men scrutinized the imagery, Withers zoomed in and identified two people in each cab, with one armed individual hunkered down in the bed of each truck. The passenger had his rifle sticking out the window in the middle truck. On the rear truck, they could make out some stored weapons as the canvas flapped in the air, revealing the payload. Both reached the same conclusion: gun runners headed west toward Iran. All the information was being sent in real-time to the command post.

Al-Tanf Garrison – Command Post

Southeastern Syria

The CP had the look of a room that was disorganized—it wasn't. Inside was a group of specialists whose duty was to gather field intelligence, directing their assets to give them the best chance of success against anyone seen as a threat to US forces in Syria. Aware they had twelve of their best men chasing terrorists across the Syrian desert, all hands were on deck to assist. In the vast expanse of the desert, situational awareness with a comprehensive view of the operating environment was crucial for keeping Americans and their allies alive.

Leaning over a detailed topographic map, Colonel Frank Spears, the base commander, worked with three others to find the optimum ambush point against the weapons convoy. The assignment was made more challenging as the terrain was flat and open, exposing anything that moved.

Using the video and travel intelligence from the Reaper crew, Spears was seeking a consensus. A boot second lieutenant was nervously taking the lead. The colonel noticed the quiver in his voice, and his finger shook as he pointed at the map. It was time to decide; they had to get this information to their twelve-man squad now.

"Sir, I know I'm the low man on the totem pole around here, but this is what I did for ten years as a park ranger: Read maps and rescue stranded people." He pointed at the map again and said, "This is the place, sir. Judging from these contour lines that are close together on either side of the dirt road, the elevation will give our men just enough concealment for the ambush." All eyes shifted to the colonel.

"I guess if you have the balls to disagree with me, Lieutenant, you are probably correct. Captain, get this information out to Ashburger immediately."

Special Operations Element

Southeastern Syria

He didn't like it, but to get ahead of the enemy convoy heading his way, Ashburger had to move faster than his desired speed which created less dust, at 32 km/h. To counter this, he had his men squeeze into just two vehicles, leaving the third one behind.

With the help of the Reaper crew and the CP, the squad arrived at the designated coordinates on the map. According to the Reaper team, they had approximately twelve minutes before the gun runners arrived. The Green Berets were deployed and ready.

Over the radio came the message they all had anticipated: "Stargazer, convoy is on you."

"Now," yelled Ashburger to his driver. Sherwood stomped on the accelerator, and the large M-ATV jumped from behind a knoll out in the middle of the dirt road just as the lead truck approached, causing the driver to slam on his brakes, stopping just a few yards before the hefty, armored vehicle. Dust from the three pickup trucks covered the scene momentarily, and nothing happened. Suddenly, armed men burst from the three trucks and took cover on the side of the road. It was like it was all rehearsed. One terrorist grabbed a

Dehlavieh anti-tank missile from the bed of the middle truck and sprinted out into the desert, taking cover behind a small berm. As the man ran, gunfire erupted from everywhere.

Ashburger yelled at his gunner, "Get that asshole with the Dehlavieh."

"Got it." With that, the gunner let loose with his M240B machine gun, walking the rounds to where the combatant was raising his anti-tank missile to fire. With huge chunks of dust and dirt flying, several rounds struck the man just as he fired, causing the missile to fly skyward just above the M-ATV.

Meanwhile, nine special ops fighters were set up along the road, firing their MK 16 SCAR-L assault rifles. The small berm they set up behind provided just enough cover as they pounded the enemy with return fire. One of the special ops soldiers was temporarily blinded by dirt from a near miss and had to hunker down for a second, but still managed to let loose with some rounds. Within a couple of minutes, silence returned to the desert as the gun runners lay dead.

Over comms: "Everyone check in—anyone hit?" Quickly, the troops answered back in the order they were trained to do. Ashburger was relieved to hear his men were all good to go. "I want Team Alpha to set up a perimeter while we check out each truck and see what we have.

Washington, check out the dead and see what you can get in the way of intelligence. The rest of you go through the trucks and watch out for possible booby traps."

Going through each pickup truck carefully, the troops uncovered a large stash of weapons, including Glocks, PK machine guns, DShK heavy machine guns, numerous RPGs, and the diamonds of the stash, several Kornet and Milan anti-tank guided missiles. After talking with HQ, Ashburger decided to drive the loot back to the base using the terrorists' pickup trucks. Intelligence gathered by Washington and others would later reveal the men were all part of Iran's IRGC.

As the squad drove back to the Al-Tanf Garrison, Ashburger debriefed himself on what he might have done better for the safety of all eleven of his men. It didn't take long—it was a near-perfect operation.

Chapter 30

Lebanon Retreat Restaurant

Dearborn, Michigan

They all arrived by Uber, dressed in their best nondescript American clothing: blue jeans and a plain shirt so as not to draw attention. The owner of Lebanon Retreat was an official from the Muslim Center of Michigan and a former Hezbollah soldier who welcomed each visitor to a secluded back room of the restaurant.

They were seated around a large round table typically used for catering. The group was led by Samir Makhlouf, who represented the Supreme Leader. In attendance were Ahmad Nadar, Umair Sabar, Umair's trusted second-in-command, Aahad Jabbour, and—taking up almost two seats—Mustafa Latif.

Samir began the meeting. " Assalamu alaikum, peace be upon you, my brothers. I have heard so much about you, Umair; I am happy to meet you. Praise Allah."

"Praise Allah" echoed around the room as the others repeated the phrase.

"Please, let me get right to the point," said Samir. "The infidels of the US have murdered many of our leaders. They have martyred Foroohar Nakhjevani and Kourosh Ormazd, and Commander Qasem Soleimani. We just received a report that the Americans killed eleven of our warriors in Syria who were just returning to their homeland. May their sacrifices be a source of inspiration for us all, and Allah bless their souls.

"Currently, there is an effort by the US to reduce the influence of Hezbollah in Lebanon and drive a wedge between us. For too many years, we have done nothing in the United States to remind the nonbelievers of the power of Allah with us as soldiers—we are now working as one to change that." Around the room were nods of agreement.

"Today, I have invited our new friends. The Prophet Muhammad taught us the importance of choosing good companions and fostering positive relationships. He has taught us in a time of need to become one. In this room, we are one with each other." More nods. Samir paid close attention to Umair and Aahad and could tell by their facial expressions that they would do what was asked of them for their country of Lebanon and Allah.

"We soon will strike at the infidels of America and ask our brothers, Umair Sabar and Aahad Jabbour, if you are with us at our task."

Umair stood up. "My brothers, I stand before you today to declare my unwavering support for Allah and His cause—our cause. I believe Allah is the ultimate source of guidance and mercy and will lead us to success against the Americans. I stand ready with Aahad and my band of Lebanese brothers to do whatever you ask of us.

"Let us make plans," said Samir, "to demonstrate to the world and our countrymen the power of our faith and our cause." The meeting lasted for two hours.

Chapter 31

The Whitney

Detroit, Michigan

As the server poured from a bottle of Sarah's favorite out-to-dinner wine, The Prisoner, a fine 2022 Red Blend, she couldn't help staring into Jessie's sparkling blue eyes. Sitting in the bay window of the elegant 1894 home, The Whitney, which had belonged to the wealthiest man in Detroit during the lumber era, she must admit she loved this Alpha fighter pilot so much. She wondered again, for the umpteenth time, if the feeling was mutual.

"So, tell me again," he said, interrupting her thoughts about him. Why are we eating at such a fine establishment and drinking this red stuff?" This was coming from a guy who had been eating Navy food for a decade and only agreed to eat here because she said she would pick up the tab, the cheap SOB.

She took a minute to answer as she breathed in all the aromas of the wine; she delighted in the nose of ripe raspberry, vanilla, and coconut, giving way to flavors of fresh and dried blackberry, pomegranate, and vanilla. She knew her wines, thanks to her dad. Meanwhile, Jessie, being a beer-drinking sort of guy, had no idea what she was doing.

"Sweetheart,"—she never called him that—"I fell in love with you five years ago when we were both in sickbay aboard the *Reagan.* When you heard me crying and came into my room, I immediately saw through my tears that you cared about me. The next two days sealed the deal for me, and now I want us to carry our relationship into the future—together. I want us to make this work despite our careers in the Navy. We must. I love you, Jessie, I always have."

Jessie had to concede that those days in sick bay when they were in adjoining rooms because of injuries received when they both ditched their aircraft into the South China Sea—changed his life. Before Sarah, flying fighters was the only thing important in his life—the faster, the better. But over the past five years, when they managed to get together—which was seldom—he felt love for this woman. It changed him. Perhaps that is why he held back; he was unsure how to proceed. This was all new to him for a guy always in charge of everything—time to engage the afterburner.

Gently taking her hand between his, looking at the only real love of his life, he let it rip like a 9-G turn. "Sarah, I have never forgotten those 48 hours together on the *Reagan* and the few times we have been together since. For the first time in my Naval life, I wanted to stay with you and not in the cockpit of my fighter. Before you, nothing would stop me from flying. But after I set eyes on you and we had our first kiss, life changed for me, for us, right up to this moment."

Looking down for a moment, then getting lost in her eyes, Jessie continued. "I'm ready to commit—to us, to our lives together. I don't know how our logistics will work out, but we can adjust and make it work. I love you so much, Sarah."

Feeling her soul ready to burst with joy, Sarah said. "I'm so happy to hear that, Jessie. I don't want to wait any longer. Let's see if we can pull this off before you return to the *Ford*."

"You mean get married—now?"

Sarah squeezed Jessie's hand even tighter, "Yes, my love, now." Just then, the waiter came and filled both their wine glasses, giving them each a moment to soak all this in.

"Perfect timing," said Jessie with a big shit-eating grin. Holding his glass, he said, "Here's to us as one; I will love you forever."

Chapter 32

Outside the Al-Tanf Garrison

Southeastern Syria

The four HESA Shahed 136 one-way attack drones were fired from Iran at precisely 0315 hours local time, 0245 in Syria. Each drone had a 100-pound warhead programmed to strike near the main gate at the US base at Al-Tanf Garrison. Fifty elite IRGC Quds led by Captain Amir Asgari were lying in wait, wearing Russian-made Ratnik-3 exoskeleton protective camouflage suits that hide the soldier's thermal signature.

"Falcon Two, Falcon One, are you in position?"

"Falcon One to Two, roger, all men accounted for and ready to strike."

"Two to One, four minutes out," said Asgari, referring to drone impact. Asgari knew full well this mission was near suicidal as the chances of surviving this one were minimal. No matter, all fifty soldiers knew it was a mission conceived and blessed by the Supreme Leader to promote the Islamic Revolution and to expand Iran's influence in the Middle East. Americans were about to get the message firsthand.

Inside the Al-Tanf Garrison

Southeastern Syria

Captain Roger Ashburger pulled his beach recliner right to the shoreline as his wife held out a drink and was about to hug him when the sound of a siren came echoing from her mouth. WTF! Shaking himself awake as he jumped out of his rack, Ashburger heard the piercing sound of sirens and from his radio squawking about incoming bogeys. Grabbing his MK-16, he headed out the door and was met by his squad of eleven other special ops men heading to their pre-assigned positions around the compound. All wore their Fusion Spiral Enhanced Night Vision goggles, which also had thermal cameras and TYR Tactical PICO armor.

Just as the men spread out to their stations, two massive explosions lit up the pitch-black sky near the front gate. There was organized bedlam everywhere as soldiers took up defensive positions, waiting for what they all expected—a ground assault on Al-Tanf.

"Stargazer to all units; do not rush the main gate. Go to your assigned positions," ordered Ashburger.

Fortunately, the newly installed micro-doppler radar targeted two of the four drones and shot them down. CP reported no other hostile drones or missiles.

Outside the Hesco barriers surrounding Al-Tanf, Asgari's men had planted explosives near the ammo storage area and the airfield. As planned, the Quds waited two minutes for the Americans to respond to the drones' attack at the front entrance, then ignited their explosives.

"Fire now," ordered Asgari as his squad prepared to breach the exposed flank of their enemy. Firing 60mm mortars to suppress fire, the specially trained troops stormed through the small gap, firing randomly as they spread out on either side of the barriers. Using thermal night-vision goggles, the Quds efficiently identified threats, firing as they moved toward numerous parked Black Hawk helicopters. Four explosive experts moved under the withering fire of their squad and quickly began planting explosives on the helos.

Adjusting the sights on his M24 sniper rife, Sergeant Hugh Anderson put the crosshairs on one of the exposed sappers and squeezed off a .308 Winchester round square on the back of his head, killing him instantly. Sliding the bolt back and chambering another round, the sniper found his second target, missing him when the soldier bent over just as Anderson squeezed the trigger. The second round didn't miss. As he prepared to shoot again, return fire rained all over his concealed position, forcing him to take cover.

On the other side of the base, Asgari and twenty-four of his Quds were being held down by devastating fire from Ashburger's squad, regular Army, and members of the Syrian Democratic Forces.

"Spotlight, Falcon One, you need to take your shot now," ordered Asgari. Spotlight knew from intel where the large ammo dump was located, but he was being held down by concentrated enemy fire. "Now," came the command from Falcon One, louder this time. Spotlight stood to get a shot off using his RPG-7 with a high-explosive warhead. Aligning the rear and front sight was tough, as bullets whizzed all around like a swarm of killer bees. Fighting against the adrenaline in his body, Spotlight pulled the firing trigger, was simultaneously hit with multiple rounds, and went down, out of the fight forever.

The RPG round partially found its mark, igniting an immediate inferno with ordnance flying, not caring who the enemy was. Tracer rounds made red streaking lines like some bizarre pyrotechnic display. Both sides had to maneuver away from the growing fireball. Night vision goggles were pushed aside, and both sides fired at anything that moved.

Just when the intensity of the battle seemed it couldn't get worse, explosions thundered as several aircraft were blown apart. By now, the heavily outnumbered Quds were being picked off like so many fuzzy-trimmed targets at an amusement park. One of these men was Captain Asgari, who was shot while pulling a wounded comrade out of the line of fire. But the damage was done. Four Black Hawk helicopters, part of the base's ammo dump, and sadly, twenty-two Allied soldiers, including one from Special Ops, were killed.

"Stargazer to all units, sweep the area, check for enemy survivors. Provide medical aid as necessary and get them to the brig. Notify me ASAP."

Despite the deaths of all his raiders, the The Supreme Leader of Iran accomplished his goal of sending a message to the world: that Lebanon and Hezbollah were again a force to be reckoned with.

Chapter 33

The White House
United States of America

President Mark Taylor looked down at the timer on the treadmill and couldn't believe it had only been eight minutes since he began his daily workout. *Why me, Lord?* he asked himself sarcastically. He could almost hear the Almighty tell him it was because his only baby, Jennie, was always after him to eat better, work out, and cut back on his drinking. Could he help it if he enjoyed the finer things like food and wine and had a hectic life? He had gained weight during the three years she lived in Sydney, Australia. Now that she was back in the US of A, he had to admit he had sure missed her. Besides, his darling saw to it that he was losing weight again—finally.

Now in his second term, the president had accomplished a resounding victory with his triumph over China in their attempt at reunifying Taiwan. The nation had embraced him for swiftly negotiating peace terms that the People's Republic of China accepted within a matter of days. With five years of uninterrupted peace between the two countries,

Taiwan carried on with its affairs without any immediate threat from its Western neighbor, at least for the time being.

Looking at his watch, the president thought he'd better cut this workout early to prepare for a thirty-minute meeting with his National Security Council. Sorry, Jennie.

Everyone stood up as the president walked into the room, and a scattering of good mornings could be heard. "Thank you. Please be seated." As he scanned the room, he was still adjusting to new faces and happy to see a few trusted advisors along for the ride in his second term. "I called this meeting today to discuss our policy with Iran and the Middle East region. I see a change in Iran with their recent moves of imposing sanctions against ninety-six Americans and their continued attacks on American troops in the Middle East, especially what just occurred at our base in Syria, where they killed American and our Allied troops. There is no doubt who did this, and the offenders must be made to pay."

Looking around the room, he saw nods of agreement. He continued. "It should go without saying I want everyone in this room to fully understand my resolve to protect and defend our citizens here and around the world against terrorism. While we sometimes have trouble agreeing on different policies and laws, by God, we are united in our resolve against any threat or provocation from Iran. We stand united in defense of our country—no discussion is needed on the severe consequences if they break any of these tenets." Giving his remarks a second to settle in, he continued, "Now I would like our Director of National Intelligence, Elena Ramirez, to bring us all up to date on Iranian intelligence. Elena."

"Thank you, Mr. President," said the DNI. "First, I want to say that it would be an egregious mistake on the part of Congress and others to put terrorism on the back burner as we turn our focus more and more to peer adversaries like China and Russia. A nuclear-empowered Iran is just as dangerous, if not more so.

"What we are witnessing is an increasingly brazen Iran using its network of proxies and hackers to target America and American citizens around the globe. These terrorists are becoming more multidimensional by adapting to new technologies, leveraging social media for recruitment and propaganda, exploiting online platforms for radicalization, and employing innovative tactics and strategies. They increasingly use encrypted communication channels to avoid detection, spread their ideologies globally, and recruit individuals from diverse backgrounds. Additionally, they seek alliances with other criminal networks, making their operations more complex and more challenging to counter.

“As our policymakers cut funding for our battle against terrorism, they need to be reminded by us in the intelligence profession that Iran's support for terrorism is legitimate and vigorous.”

The DNI continued to make eye contact with everyone in the room to signify the importance of what she was putting forth. "Just last year, the Justice Department indicted three Iranian nationals, charging them in a plot to attack and extort money from hundreds of victims here in the US. This included everything from police departments to a children's hospital. The director of the FBI called the activity 'just the tip of the iceberg.'

"Lastly, our administration should support the current protest inside of Iran. This is not new. In 2009, the Green Revolution saw hundreds of thousands of Iranians protest the fraudulent re-election of then-Iranian president Mahmoud Ahmadinejad. The clerical regime understood the importance of quelling these protests, as proved when as many as fifteen hundred demonstrators were killed. Recently, there were protests involving thousands calling for reforming the governing system and dismantling the entire regime. Protestors were bold enough to shout, 'Where's my vote?' and 'Death to the dictator.'

"We need to adopt a policy to strengthen our response to the existing faults of the regime while supporting the protestors in creating a government that forsakes the quest for nuclear weapons and stops their regional aggression. The US should address every aspect of disruption to the country, big or small, and not just contest Iran's nuclear program."

As the meeting continued, it was clear to everyone on the NSC that changes were necessary to contain Iran's regional ambitions and strengthen US security at home. No matter what was happening on the national scene, with peer powers flaunting their ideology worldwide, terrorism would continue to be at the forefront of threats to the nation. It's like a pesky bug that refuses to go away, even when swatted.

Looking around the room but letting his eyes settle on his Secretary of Defense, George Mitchell, still with him from his first term, President Taylor said, "George, I want you to develop a strategy for an air strike on infrastructure facilities used by groups affiliated with Iran's Revolutionary Guards Corps. It's time to send a message to those who wish people harm in the Middle East. I want it ASAP."

Chapter 34

Rouge Park

Detroit, Michigan

Bouncing along in Sabar's raised red Dodge Ram pickup truck, the three new terrorists-in-training were following precise directions given to them by Ahmad Nadar. They were headed to the Rouge Park electrical transmission substation. Behind the wheel was Umair Sabar. Riding shotgun was his second in command, Aahad Jabbour. A third man—called "BM" for Big Man, as he was six-seven, 280 pounds, and no fat—was in the back.

"Turn left on Parkland," said BM, who had the directions written down on a piece of paper. After a few moments, "That's it," pointing to the fenced-in area surrounding the electrical substation with prominent "No Trespassing" signs posted every ten yards.

Parking under some trees across the road and ensuring no one was in the area, the three men got out, walking up the gravel driveway to the locked gate. BM was part of the strike team because of his first-hand knowledge of power stations currently operated by Detroit Edison. He was also a radicalized American citizen of Lebanese descent and detested everything about this country. Like most in the

Warren Bros, he had been persecuted his entire twenty-eight years and now identified as Muslim, following the preachings of Allah and the Supreme Leader.

As the three men were going over the plan with BM, reviewing exactly what part of the substation they would target, two runners approached from the wooded running trail that snaked its way through the entire park.

Sarah stopped Jessie in his tracks. "Wait a minute. I recognize that truck; it belongs to the guys who were at the range the other day. I recognize the plate." Looking through the trees, they saw three men pointing at something through the fence. "Something's not right here," Sarah said.

"Roger that," said Jessie, "they look like fucking terrorists setting up their next target."

Just then, Sabar saw them, "Hey, you," yelled Sabar, "this is posted property, and you have no right being here." With that, the three men reached for something under their jackets and began to move toward the two Naval officers.

"Time to unass the area," said Jessie. Without a second thought, the two took off in the opposite direction, and both were quickly swallowed up by the trees lining the running path.

"Shit, fuck," said Sabar, "we sure didn't need that."

"It's no biggie," said Aahad. "They were just two runners with no idea what we were doing. Let's finish and get out of here."

BM said, "They look like the two that were at the 10-Ring a few days ago. I don't know about you guys, but to me, they look like feds. And that is a biggie."

"Good point. Let's get to the main parking area," said Sabar. "If it's who you say they are, they drive a new Porsche. That shouldn't be hard to spot, and we can see what they're up to."

Sarah and Jessie hauled ass back to the Porsche, thinking the three men might be coming after them. Already, they were speculating that these three men they saw at the firing range with a powerful rifle might be planning something at the power station. Neither one believed in coincidences—things happened for a reason.

As the two were about to enter the wide-open parking lot, they heard and then saw the huge red Dodge truck roaring down the street and screeching into the parking lot. Jessie pushed Sarah back, and they both jumped behind a tree. "Shit," said Jessie, "that's our boys."

"Do you think we should call the police," said Sarah.

"And tell them what," said Jessie, "that we saw three guys outside the fence at a power plant—pointing. No, let's lay low, and if they mess with the car or see us, we call 911."

They saw the truck pull in behind the Porsche. From their vantage point, it appeared that one of the passengers wrote down the license plate number. Then some big guy got out, looked into the car, around the surrounding parking lot. It seemed he was staring right at them. Both got closer to the tree. Just then, a park ranger came by and started down the lane where the truck was illegally parked. Seeing this, BM got back in, and the truck drove out of the parking lot.

"I sure don't like the looks of this," said Jessie. "These assholes are up to something, and it ain't good."

"Let's give it a minute and see if they come back," said Sarah. After a long ten minutes, the two got into the Porsche and headed home, with Sarah checking her mirrors nonstop. Both agreed they needed to report this to the authorities.

Chapter 35

CNN

Washington, DC

Cutting away from a piece on the postal rate increase, the well-dressed news anchor put a stern look on his face and reported: "We have breaking news. We are going to the White House, where the Secretary of Defense, George Mitchell, is about to make an announcement."

Instantly, the feed went to the camera at the White House as Mitchell was walking up to the podium in the Press Briefing Room.

Behind him, several generals came into the frame, including the chairman of the Joint Chiefs of Staff. All carried themselves in a no-bullshit kind of way. The American flag on the SecDef's lapel momentarily caught the light and reflected back toward the millions of Americans watching the feed. All forty-nine seats in the press room were crammed with reporters. Secretary Mitchell began:

> At the direction of President Taylor, I authorized US Central Command forces to conduct precision airstrikes in eastern Syria, against targets used by groups affiliated with Iran's Islamic Revolutionary Guards Corps. The airstrikes were conducted in

> response to yesterday's attack at our base in eastern Syria, Al-Tanf Garrison, where twenty-two Allied troops were killed and several aircraft were destroyed. All attackers were killed.
>
> As President Taylor has said many times, the US will take all necessary measures to defend our people and will always respond at a time and place of our choosing. No group will strike our troops with impunity.
>
> Our thoughts and prayers are with the families and loved ones of the soldiers killed and those wounded in the unprovoked attack.

With that, Mitchell closed his folder as cries of "Mr. Secretary" broke out from the assembled press, and the entourage left one of the most significant stages in the world as tensions in the Middle East reached a new level of seriousness.

Chapter 36

FBI Field Office

Detroit, Michigan

Both agents were on their second cup of coffee, going over the Nadar case, when the phone rang. It was a welcome relief as it seemed the investigation was going nowhere.

"FBI Field Office, Agent Jennings, how can I help you?"

"Hello, Agent Jennings. My name is Sarah Freeman, and I'm currently on leave from the Navy."

"Why, thank you for your service, Ms. Freeman."

"Please call me Sarah."

"Sure thing, Sarah. What's up?

"If you don't mind," said Sarah, "please let me start from the top."

"Of course."

"A few days ago, my boyfriend and I were at the 10-Ring Shooting Range..." Sarah went on to explain the high-powered rifle, her impressions of the men, and the frightening encounter with those same men.

"Did you happen to get the plate of the truck?" asked Harley.

"Sure did." After giving the plate number to Jennings, Sarah noticed the agent showed much more interest in her story.

"If you don't mind, Sarah, I want to bring in my partner, Ali Mohsen. I am putting you on speaker."

"Hi, Sarah," said Ali. "Can you describe the pickup truck again to ensure we have this correct?"

She did. There was a moment of silence on the phone, but she could hear whispering in the background.

"Whom is the Porsche registered to?" asked Jennings.

"It's my dad's car."

"Okay, give us a moment, and we will call you back. We want to go over a few things."

"Sure. Is there anything wrong?"

"We will call you right back," Jennings said, and hung up.

The two agents looked at each other for a moment, each taking in what they had just heard. Jennings spoke first. "Okay, get the boss in here, and let's quickly formulate a plan. This has a bad vibe to it."

Five minutes later, the SAC was brought up to speed, and he asked the two questions they all had on their minds: How do we ensure the safety of witnesses and family, and what are the Warren Bros planning? Both questions were troublesome.

"First," said Williamson, "I want 24/7 protective surveillance on the wit's home in Hamtramck. It appears that the gang is planning a hit on the Rouge Park power station. We can't let that happen. I want video surveillance set up immediately and have it monitored. Finally, I want eyes on Sabar, and hopefully, that will lead us to Nadar. Any questions?"

"These assignments will stretch us pretty thin; any chance we can get some temporary assistance?" asked Jennings.

"Good point," said the SAC, "I will make that happen. Now let's get back to our wit and let her know what is going down."

Chapter 37

Warren Bros
Dearborn, Michigan

Umair Sabar grew up in the streets of Dearborn after moving from Lebanon with his mom. A man who commands a gang, engages in bitter fights with rival gangs, and survives countless encounters with the police quickly learns the rules for survival. Your gut tells you when something doesn't fit or seems out of place. You trust no one and believe only what you can verify.

Just days after the encounter with the feds or cops or whatever they were at Rouge Park, he began to see patterns that were out of the ordinary. Cars that appeared to be following him would turn off, only to be replaced a few blocks later with another car that seemed to be interested in his route. When he parked and was doing his thing, he picked up on the telltale signs of being shadowed. At home, when he would burst out of his house for a run, he saw signs he was being watched.

He had a job to do for his new best friend, Ahmad, and he would not let him or the cause down. Praise be to Allah; he will find the way. And that way was to level the playing field. He needed insurance to complete his mission of taking out the power station at Rouge Park.

Hamtramck, Michigan

Sarah was happy. She and Jessie, the love of her life, had finally agreed that it was time to move their relationship to the next level. After five years of a hit-and-miss courtship because of their careers, it was time to pull the pin and get married. Yikes, she thought, married. She still had some adjusting to do, but her love for Jessie sure didn't.

Although her dad was steadily slipping away—with who knows what, the doctors sure as hell didn't—she was delighted that on his good days, she could still see the love for life in his eyes. He even accepted Jessie as part of the family, which made her especially happy. Even better, today, the two were going fishing together over at Milliken Harbor. A guys' day out.

The only thing—and it was a thing—was the constant FBI presence around the house and when she and Jessie went out. It had been over a week since the encounter at the park, and they were adjusting, but it was a hassle. When you have fought in a war and almost ate it, crap like this seemed insignificant.

When Sarah saw her dad come out of his bedroom, she had to admit he looked pretty good in his flannel shirt and the old fishing hat he had worn for as long as she could remember. Jessie was wearing a Go Navy t-shirt and a blue US Naval Aviation hat. They stopped and checked each other out.

"Where's the tackle box," said Jessie, "we don't want to forget that."

"It's in the garage, probably buried by who knows what, as it's been a while since this old man went fishing."

"Roger that."

As Jessie walked by Sarah, he whispered, "You be a good girl now, and don't get in any trouble."

"Who me? Of course not," she said with a smile and then pecked him on the cheek. "I love you."

"Love you too."

Sarah's dad said, "Okay, if I can separate you two lovebirds, it's time to get going. See you on the flip side, sweetheart."

As they walked out the door, Sarah couldn't believe she had some time to herself. She went to her room and threw on an old, battered E-2 Hawkeye t-shirt and some running shorts. Time for her run and a gratifying cup of java when she finished.

As she walked out the front, she made eye contact with the two FBI agents parked in the neighbor's driveway and pumped her arms to show them she was off for her run. From the car, the lights blinked. Today, she decided to keep it short and run the 2.8-mile City Walk route.

Warming up on Denton Street, she picked up the pace as she ran down Joseph Campeau, turning left down the one-way street, Andrus. The two agents knew this route and drove past Andrus, as they would have been going the wrong way, and kept going down Campau, planning to pick her up in two blocks at Danforth Steet. Easy-peasy.

As Sarah ran down Andrus, she turned right down the alley as she always did, giving her a break from traffic. As soon as she made her turn, she saw a black van parked partially inside an old red brick garage. As she was digesting this, one extremely large man jumped out of the garage, wrapping his huge arms around her and stopping her in her tracks. Instantly, someone threw a hood over her head, and she was thrown into the back of the van. The door quickly slammed shut, and she heard a voice from the front, "Don't say a word, bitch, or I will plant a 9-millimeter round in that pretty face of yours. Understand?"

At first, she thought of fighting back but quickly decided to play along and wait for her opportunity. She answered in a very subdued voice, “Yes.”

Efficiently, the van turned back down Andrus and went past the adjoining alley, coming out on Grayling and turning right down the one-way street.

As the FBI agents came up on Danforth, they pulled to the right, knowing she would be there in seconds. When a minute passed and they didn’t see Sarah, the passenger agent jumped from the car and sprinted in the direction of where Sarah should be. Standing there, looking down the alley and up and down the street, he knew they had screwed up. As the other agent pulled up, he yelled, “Get on the radio and put out an officer needs help call and get DPD here. Fuck!”

Down at the lake, Jessie was quietly bullshitting with Sarah’s dad when the two agents in the plain car that had been following them jumped from their vehicle with guns drawn. Quickly but efficiently, the two fishermen were pushed into the back seat as the car squealed away from the area. “Sorry, men, Sarah is missing, and we can’t take chances with you two anymore.”

“What,” yelled Jessie, “missing?”

Chapter 38

Muslim Center of Michigan

Dearborn, Michigan

At precisely 10 p.m., there was a knock at the rear door to Samir Makhlouf's living quarters at the Muslim Center of Michigan. Samir's bodyguard, Mustafa Latif, answered the door and let in Ahmad Nadar. "Assalamu alaikum, peace be upon you."

"Wa alaykum as-salam, and peace be upon you too." Both men embraced with mutual respect, a far cry from their first meeting. Samir sat in a chair away from his desk and offered Ahmad the seat in front of him. Latif left the room.

"I have heard from our Supreme Leader. He wishes us his blessings, Masha Allah, in our mission for Allah and our country. What we are about to discuss is only known by you, me, our Supreme Leader, and Allah. It must be so."

"So be it."

"Let the blessed day be July 4th, for maximum impact to the infidels of America. It is the day that they celebrate their independence, the day they signed the forms in that very building, Independence Hall. Destroying this iconic symbol of American democracy will demonstrate that Allah is the supreme and ultimate deity in Islam and the world."

"I stand ready," said Ahmad. "What are the particulars of the mission?"

"You will depart June 30th by car, which we will provide. One of our operatives in Philadelphia will contact you. He only knows he will be your backup and assistant on the mission, which he knows nothing about. You will stay with him. You will only spend cash, which we will give you. No credit card, ever."

After a nod from Ahmad, Samir continued. "I will provide you with your M72s today. They will be in heavy-duty cases that look like video camera containers. You will also be provided with a PC-9 Zoaf sidearm. We will leave the time and launching area of the attack to your discretion for July 4th. We know you have a plan."

Ahmad had a plan but wanted to keep it to himself; there was no better security than just him knowing. He saw Samir had more to add.

"And one more thing, Ahmad. While we understand it would be more advantageous for you to fire one warhead and escape, we pray to Allah that you will fire both, ensuring the complete destruction of the building and even the Liberty Bell."

"I will do my best for you, and my country, but especially for Allah."

Chapter 39

Joint Terrorism Task Force (JTTF)

FBI Field Office, Detroit, Michigan

"Thank you for getting here on such short notice," said the Special Agent in Charge, John Williamson, to a full room. "Let's get started. Two days ago, a witness to a possible attack on an electrical power station was kidnapped off the streets despite our supervision. Sarah Freeman is on leave from the Navy, taking care of her ailing father. At 1530 hours, she and Jessie Hampton, her boyfriend, also on leave from the Navy, were running in Rouge Park when they happened on three men of Lebanese descent who are members of the street gang Warren Bros. We have positively identified two of the men as Umair Sabar, the leader of the gang, and his top associate, Aahad Jabbour." As the SAC was talking, PowerPoint slides were shown on a large screen. In the room were sixty-two members of different law enforcement agencies giving their undivided attention.

"The two wits observed a truck that Freeman recognized from the 10-Ring Shooting Range, where the same men were firing a high-powered rifle next to their shooting lane. The truck is described as a raised red Dodge Ram with oversized off-road tires. He gave the plate number. Here are some photos she took of the men. She also heard them arguing about different types of rounds and, specifically, which ones could penetrate thick metal.

"She said the truck was parked under some trees and not in the facility's driveway. The three men were next to the fence at the Rouge Park electrical transmission substation, pointing into the facility. After they saw our two wits, they appeared to be drawing handguns from their waistbands, but neither wit saw any weapons displayed. The two ran back to where their car was parked, but the men had returned to their truck and driven to the parking lot, so our wits hid in the wooded area. They saw one of the men, suspect three, get out and look into their car. It also appeared that one of them wrote down the license plate."

A senior officer from the Michigan State Police asked, "How did they know which car was theirs?"

"Yes, the suspects saw them get into a newer model Porsche at the shooting range—the same car they drove to the park. When a park ranger happened by, the suspects took off.

"From video cameras in the vicinity of the kidnapping, we were able to identify the suspects' vehicle as a newer model Ford Transit cargo van, black, with temporary plates we could not identify. Surveillance from the Tip a Few bar, their hang-out, has not revealed any sign of the suspects."

A Wayne County Sheriff's Office deputy raised his hand and asked, "Any idea why they would have kidnapped Freeman and not her boyfriend, or why they even singled her out?"

Agent Ali Mohsen jumped in on this one. "Our investigation indicates they may believe that our two wits are some type of cops, and were surveilling them. They are acting very hinky like something is up. With them linked to Nadar, and his surveillance of Independence Hall, we think we have the potential of a major terrorist attack."

"Thank you, Agent Mohsen," Williamson said. Turning back to the assembled lawmen, he continued, "Let me present our Director, Robert Zalinski, here to give us all perspective from Washington. Director."

"Thank you, John. I agree with Agent Mohsen's comment; we have a serious potential for a major terrorist attack on our country. Everyone, every agency is on board with us in putting these extremists behind bars. Today, the attorney general issued arrest warrants for Ahmad Nadar, Umair Sabar, and Samir Makhlouf, who is working out of the Muslim Center of Michigan. We will be moving on Makhlouf soon.

"I have been working closely with DNI, Cybersecurity and Infrastructure Security Agency, JTTF, local law enforcement, Homeland, and scores of people from our agency. We are putting the squeeze on these terrorists, and we must stop them before they act, using whatever means necessary. I am working with our field office in Philadelphia and the National Park Service to defend our ground at Independence Hall. Should these terrorists attempt an attack on our symbol of democracy, they will not succeed."

He had the complete attention of every man and woman in the room. To a person, they knew this was a big one, and they could not fail. The Director read this loud and clear and continued. "The stakes are high. We are dealing with an extraordinary situation demanding the utmost from each of us. Failure is not an option. We have unity in purpose and can succeed if we all work together and get our job done. Can I count on you?"

Like a Friday night high school football rally, the room erupted with a resounding, "Yes, sir!"

Chapter 40

Undisclosed Location

Freeman had met some dummies in her life, but these yahoos took the prize. For reasons only they knew, the dipshits believed she was a cop or federal agent. They accused her of staking them out, following them to the target range, and again to the power station.

Sarah was apprehensive. It'd been two days since her kidnapping. She was not concerned about herself so much, but about her father and Jessie. She knew they would be worried sick, and there was no telling what Jessie was up to. If he got a sniff of where these assholes were, he would kill them all without giving it a second thought. That picture would've made her feel better, but for the bad guys ratcheting up their interrogation.

BM, a name she learned as the three men talked to each other, seemed to have taken a liking to her. "Listen, Sarah, why don't you tell my two friends what you reported to your superiors? They don't believe you are in the Navy. I don't know what they are up to, but they said there could be no leaks."

"Listen closely, BM. I like you; I don't see you rotting away in prison for the rest of your life for kidnapping me. You are just a bystander, with time to bring this to a safe conclusion. I promise you that if you can get me out of here in one piece, I will protect you and ensure the authorities understand that. What—"

"BM, what the fuck are you doing?" said Umair. "Don't talk to the bitch, bro, how many times have I told you?"

"Sorry, boss, she just wanted a glass of water."

"I don't care if she wants a steak dinner, don't talk to her—period."

"I must say," said Sarah, "that sure sounds delicious."

"Shut up, bitch, before I cap you."

"So violent," she smirked.

At that, Umair rushed over to where she was sitting with her hands handcuffed behind a chair and smacked her with his right hand, knocking her backward onto the floor. Blood immediately began oozing from what felt like a broken nose.

"Big man, aren't you? Hit a lady with her hands tied behind her back."

Umair then gave her a kick in the ribs. "Listen, you bitch, I'm done messing with you. Either you tell me who you work for and what you told them about us, or I beat you to death and throw your body in the Rouge River."

The kick really unnerved her, but she still managed to moan out, "Fuck you. I am Lieutenant Commander Sarah Freeman, serial N251CA6472—"

With that, Umair yelled, "BM, sit her the fuck up so I can smash her face again." BM did as he was told and was too afraid to say anything to this pretty girl, who didn't deserve any of this. "Now listen, bitch—"

"I'm sorry, my name is Sarah Freeman." That earned her a punch in the face.

"Cute," said Umair, "but me killing you might not seem so charming. Maybe you are in the Navy, as you say, but I believe they also have an intelligence service, and you could be part of that, spying on us. Tell me what I want to know, and I will let you go after this is over. Choose not to, well…you can figure that out."

"Let me break this down again for you, and tell me if I go too fast."—Slap—"I guess I was going too fast."

"Just shut the fuck up," said Umair. "Who do you work for?"

"The US Navy—carrier pilot." The gang leader struck her, knocking her backward again. This time her head hit the ground with a loud *smack*. The last thing Sarah saw was Amair's big fist heading toward her face, then blackness.

Chapter 41

Independence Hall

Philadelphia, Pennsylvania

July 4th was about as busy as it got at Independence Hall. It seemed the entire nation had to get to Philadelphia to celebrate America's birthday. This would be Kordell Jackson's second go-around. The ex-cop was still recovering from the death of his partner—but getting stronger each day. It was amazing to him how his wife was beginning to forgive him for his drunken treatment of the family while he was fighting his demons.

Being a security cop at the Hall was not what he pictured himself doing. He was born to be a street cop, but for right now, it was a perfect fit. He was still healing.

The team of security experts were gathered in a large conference room, going over the possibility of a terrorist strike on the iconic site. Speaking was the Special Agent in Charge of the FBI Philadelphia office. "Thanks to the observations of Mr. Jackson, we feel quite sure of some type of terrorist attack, led by an American citizen, Ahmad Nadar. We are asking that you use extreme diligence, keeping a sharp eye for anything that looks out of the ordinary. We have handed out the special phone number to call and the radio call sign for the mission commander. We will all use the same radios and network. In your packet, you also have a photograph of Nadar and his known associates.

"You will see members of our FBI SWAT team in the area to supplement your security. We will have other assets in the vicinity for added support. Those remain classified."

The SAC was referring to a battery of Avenger Air Defense systems, each consisting of eight Stinger missiles and two M3 .50 caliber machine guns. They were secretly placed atop a 17-story building near Independence Hall. The battery was specifically designed to defend against low-level air attacks such as drones and small aircraft. The missiles are infrared-guided and have a range of two miles. This is the same type of system that sits atop buildings near the White House.

"Additionally, the Philadelphia Police Department will have officers patrolling the area, both in uniform and plainclothes. While deployment has already begun, we will have maximum readiness beginning on July 2nd.

"Listen, this is a serious threat that can never be allowed to materialize. Let's all work as a team to protect this symbol of freedom for our great country. Thank you."

Kordell Jackson asked to be assigned random patrol of the area during the major deployment. He had his hunches about Nadar and wanted to be able to act on them should the need arise. While he respected the FBI, he was like most cops; they feel the streets belong to them, and that they are best adapted to handle them and the predators that call them home. For him, a terrorist was no different than a gangbanger or any other thug.

Chapter 42

Three years earlier

Congregation Beth Israel Synagogue

Colleyville, Texas

"Everyone put your hands in the air, or I will kill you," screamed Malik Faisal Akram, a 44-year-old British Pakistani. "Do as I say, and you will be spared." As he talked, Akram waved his Taurus G2C pistol around in the air while continually making threats.

Only four congregation members were in the room, a single expansive area with vibrant stained-glass windows, and he quickly gathered them together. One of the four hostages was Jeffrey R. Cohen, who smartly dialed 911 on his cell phone and then discreetly set it down, glass first. It was 10:41 a.m. When the Colleyville Police Department received the call, they immediately dispatched a unit that arrived a few minutes later and discerned it was a hostage situation. Using protocols already set for such a contingency, the police chief ensured the call went out to the Texas Department of Public Safety and the Federal Bureau of Investigation.

Eventually, over two hundred local, state, and federal law enforcement officers responded to the scene. Included in this number were seventy FBI hostage negotiators and rescue agents who flew in from Quantico, Virginia. Leading the Hostage Rescue Team was Todd Wilkerson, a Marine combat veteran from West Virginia.

After Akram let three of the hostages go, the negotiations broke down. The order came to breach the building and rescue the remaining hostage.

Wilkerson gathered his fourteen HRT members on the far side of the building to go over the entry plan. "Okay, we have the perimeter secured. Our job is to make entry and rescue the hostage, who right now is seated about fifteen feet from the suspect, who is seated near the front entrance. Bingo and I will take the lead. As we toss the flashbang into the room, we move fast to protect the hostage and neutralize the suspect. This is straight-up, men, like we have rehearsed thousands of times. Any questions? Okay, move out."

Wilkerson led his squad of FBI agents the way he had been leading men since the Marine Corps and even before that as a captain in the Charleston Police Department's Police Explorer program. He was a no-nonsense guy who gained the respect of those around him through his actions, self-confidence, and positivity. When you first meet this six-foot-two man, you instantly know you will follow him wherever he takes you. Today was no different.

As they rounded the corner to enter the temple, Wilkerson threw one flashbang toward where the suspect was seated. The bright light and concussion from the M84 temporally blinded him. Several agents rushed toward the hostage, taking him down to the ground and covering his body as Wilkerson and Bingo saw Akram raise his gun. Both agents fired from their 1911 .45 pistols, killing Akram. Mission accomplished. The hostage was not injured, and the suspect was neutralized.

Chapter 43

Present Time

FBI Field Office

Detroit, Michigan

"I called this special meeting of the JTTF to go over the details for serving a search warrant on the Muslim Center here in Dearborn," said John Williamson. "We have been in a reaction mode to the terrorists here and in Philadelphia. The Director wants us to be more proactive to prevent whatever these extremists have planned. The consensus is that the Warren Bros are working through Makhlouf and Nadar for a strike here in our area, probably as a diversionary tactic to whatever is planned for Independence Hall. We need to disrupt their plans and start getting these terrorists off the streets. That will start tomorrow. I want to turn this meeting over to our lead agents on this case, Jennings and Mohsen. Guys."

Jennings took the lead. "Working with the attorney general, we have a warrant for the arrest of Samir Makhlouf, a highly placed agent in the Iranian government working with Hezbollah and the Islamic Revolutionary Guard. Also named in the warrant is Mustafa Latif, a Quds soldier from the IRG assigned as Makhlouf's bodyguard. Latif is highly trained and judging from past experiences in this type of situation, he will not come along easily. He is a very serious threat."

Mohsen took the lead. "I have worked on this case since the beginning. In one operation, we witnessed a meeting between Makhlouf and Umair Sabar. I followed them into the mosque, where the two men hid in the library. There, I met Latif, who played the role of librarian. Yeah, right." Some chuckles. "He told me the two men were not in the library, but I got a glimpse of them in the back rows.

"Makhlouf is the key to operations in the United States, and this is a critical mission to take him out of play. I want to introduce Todd Wilkerson, lead agent of our HRT team, who will have command of this warrant service. Agent Wilkerson."

"Thank you. This is a critical mission to get ahead of these terrorist operations here in our own country. Without a doubt, this terrorist threat has the potential of becoming another 9/11—and that's not going to happen on my watch. Taking these two players out of the equation will interrupt their flow of information and operational capability.

"Our intelligence from inside the mosque indicates that Makhlouf and Latif have a secluded residence in the rear basement area with an access door on the exterior of the building. We will have two teams. One will operate from the front entrance with the assistance of the Imam, who will let us in. From there, the team will move forward to the location at the mosque's rear. Bingo will lead that group." The big man nodded to the room.

"I will lead Team Two, who will enter from the back door. This is a knock-and-announce warrant, but we go in in tactical formation. We breach the door if we get no reply in a few seconds. We will have air support keeping an eye on the proceedings. I want DPD to secure the perimeter so no one can enter or depart. The meet-up is in the parking lot of Ralphs at 0400 hours. We go in at precisely 0500 hours. Questions? Okay, keep tight lips on this; we sure as hell don't want to give them a heads-up to our arrival. Good, let's do this."

Chapter 44

Muslim Center of Michigan

Dearborn, Michigan

The mobile command post was set up as planned. It was in a corner of the Ralphs parking lot near the mosque but out of sight. Jennings and Mohsen had overall command and decided to go with Team Two. Wilkerson was in the lead. DPD secured the perimeter. Two FBI snipers were set up in strategic locations with eyes on the front and rear of the building.

A few minutes before five, Bingo was at the front of the mosque with his team members. “One in position, no church official yet.”

“Roger, Two in position. Let me know when you are ready to enter.”

“One, roger. We have our escort.”

“Two, roger. Waiting for your update.”

“One, roger,” Bingo stated matter-of-factly. “Moving now. All quiet. In position.”

“One, announce your presence.” Simultaneously, both team leaders knocked loudly and yelled, “FBI, we have a search warrant. Open the door immediately with your hands in the air." Everyone's hearts were beating so hard they could almost use the sound of their heartbeats to count out the five seconds they had agreed to wait.

Bingo smashed open the door a split second before Wilkerson, tearing it from its hinges. As Team One entered the mosque and spread out in the prayer room, Bingo saw a huge man running toward them, screaming, "Praise Allah!" Just then, there was an enormous explosion, instantly killing Bingo and the agent behind him. The fireball was so intense the other four men were blown backward into the hall of the mosque, unconscious.

At that same instant, as Team Two was about to use the V12 Tactical Breaching tool, the door was blown outward, striking Wilkerson and the men behind him, violently knocking them to the ground. Jennings and Mohsen were well behind the HRT and were left standing. Both agents rushed toward the large hole where the door used to be, sneaking a tactical glance inside. What they saw would haunt them for a lifetime. Parts of bodies were splattered all over the room, giving it a spine-chilling red tint. Both agents saw what was left of three men: the two FBI agents and, apparently, one of the terrorists, a very big man who had to be Latif. No Makhlouf.

Jennings was on the radio. "Multiple agents down, request assistance and MedEvac. Send as many ambulances as you can muster. Do not let anyone out of the building. If seen, detain them immediately. Use caution, as Suspect One is not in custody. Unknown location." As he finished his transmission, he could hear sirens that were quickly washed out by the *whop-whop-whop* of a UH-60 helicopter as it came down in the parking lot. Two FBI agents jumped out and sprinted over to the back of the building to check for the wounded. By then, Wilkerson was shaking off the shock of the blast and felt like he could carry on. "Get inside and check on Team One." As they ran, Wilkerson attempted to follow but was stopped by Mohsen. "Wait a minute, Todd, let them do their job. Wait here, we got this." Wilkerson started to complain but took a knee to gather himself up. As he did so, the two agents ran past him to their helicopter and retrieved a stretcher. Within minutes, the men were carrying out a seriously wounded agent from Team One. Wilkerson looked up but couldn't even recognize the man, whose face—part of it missing—was covered in blood. A few minutes later, the large helicopter was taking off for the hospital, which had been advised of the operation and had emergency personnel standing by.

The SAC arrived from the command post and found his two agents in charge. Looking at both men, he was amazed at how well they were functioning despite everything that just went down, but he needed answers. "What happened?"

Mohsen answered, "As we were making our entry, a huge explosion knocked most of the team to the ground. The door and debris were flying all over the place. No warning. We did a quick survey, and it appears Latif set off a bomb when Team One entered. We need to secure the building and begin a search for Makhlouf, room by room. I was just about to issue that order."

"Sure thing, Ali, don't let me interfere."

Ali turned his back to Williamson and quickly relayed commands to gather a search team with the area's surviving HRT members and backup officers.

While he was broadcasting, medics were arriving and treating the wounded. Sirens could be heard coming and going.

Wilkerson was now up and functioning. "I got this, Ali. I will meet the newly assembled team to begin the search." Both Ali and Jennings saw blood coming from the ears of Wilkerson but did not stop the man from getting the terrorist who had killed and wounded his men—his brothers. As he moved out, news helicopters began circling the area like so many vultures. Reports from the perimeter indicated the officers had difficulty keeping the reporters out of the area as they found weaknesses in the police lines and wiggled their way inside the church. One photographer managed to get a shot of the blood-soaked room before he was discovered. That graphic single frame of film was uploaded to his news desk and was on the internet for the world to see within minutes. When discovered by the authorities, it was taken down, but not before it was seen by millions.

The search for Makhlouf was negative.

In one of the darkest days in FBI history, three agents died, and one agent would later be medically discharged. The war on terror, while pushed to the back burner by some in Washington, proved what a threat it remained to the nation's security.

Chapter 45

Interstate 76

Philadelphia, Pennsylvania

Traveling along Interstate 76 on the outskirts of Philadelphia in a late model, unexceptional Chevy Impala, Ahmad Nadar was deep in his thoughts about the technical aspects of his plan to blow up Independence Hall. The car he was driving was registered with a bogus name and address, Carlos West of Dearborn, and Ahmad had ID to match. In the trunk were the precise tools for the mission: two M72 weapons with anti-structure warheads. The cases were marked with video stickers from a non-existent production company in Dearborn.

Careful not to go over or under the speed limit, and obeying all other traffic laws, Ahmad was gradually making his way to the Philadelphia participant's home. He had received a text on his secure phone just that morning, with directions to where he would be spending the next few nights. Ahmad thought of the man as a participant because although the man was not a conspirator and knew nothing about the upcoming mission, he was providing Ahmad with a place to stay in Philadelphia. An extremely small group of terrorists, as he was taught, limits the probability of anyone discovering his plan. Working alone on the mission was even better for his welfare. All those months in Iran and Lebanon taught him so much; he would forever be thankful to Allah for allowing him to complete the task.

Getting off the freeway onto a service street as his GPS directed him to do, he rounded a long, sweeping curve. Up in front of him was a line of cars that the police had stopped. His first survival instinct was to rapidly turn around and head in the opposite direction. But just as quickly, his training took over. He knew he should not draw attention to himself. He fell into line.

When it was his turn, he had his window down and was greeted by a serious but friendly officer. "Hello, I'm Officer Grabowski of the Philadelphia Police Department. Registration and driver's license, please." While Ahmad retrieved the documents, he heard the officer say. "For the safety of our community, we have set up a DUI checkpoint to find and get impaired drivers off our roads."

"Yes, sir, I'm all about that. My brother was killed by a drunk driver three years ago. I donate to Mothers Against Drunk Drivers every Christmas in his memory."

"Well, then you shouldn't mind if I ask you if you have had anything to drink tonight."

"Not on your life, sir," said Ahmad.

"What about drugs, have you taken any today, or might you perhaps be carrying drugs in your car?"

This caught Ahmad off guard; he never thought of that. He hesitated. "Sir, I'm against putting anything like that into my body. I'm a pure soul."

"Sir, please pull over to the right. I have a few more questions and don't want to hold up the line."

"Yes, sir."

As he pulled into the spot he was ordered to, the first thing Ahmad noticed was the bright lights shining down, illuminating the area like it was daytime. He decided it was time to tactfully challenge the decision by the police officer. He didn't like where this was heading.

"Officer Grabowski, I made it clear I have not been drinking or taking drugs. I object to this unlawful detention."

"Sorry, sir, but I do have probable cause to search your car based on your demeanor. Now, please get out of the car." Ahmad started to complain but then thought better of it.

As Ahmad exited the car, a second officer approached to guard him. Grabowski immediately started going through the interior of the Chevy. The second officer said nothing but kept his shooting hand resting near his 9-mm automatic pistol. Both officers had received a briefing about a possible terrorist attack on Independence Hall, and this man fit the general description.

"Nothing, Joe."

"Sir, would you please open the trunk," said Grabowski.

Ahmad hesitated again, knowing just what the trunk contained.

"While I definitely don't agree with your handling of this situation, I have nothing to hide." He opened the trunk.

As Officer Grabowski looked in the trunk, he and the second officer were ready for anything, with their hands touching their sidearms. "What's in the cases," asked Officer Grabowski. Ahmad was prepared for this one.

Ahmad handed the officers a business card that matched the tags on the video cases, with the same fictitious name as on his bogus license. The officers took a minute to check it out:

TRAVEL VIDEOS BY CARLOS

"This is the video equipment I use to produce programs for different travel stations. I'm here to video the events around the city for July 4th."

Grabowski looked over his shoulder and noticed two more cars lining up behind them. Fuck it, he thought, time to move on. Slamming the trunk shut, he said, "Thank you, Carlos, for your cooperation; you are free to go and drive safely."

Without a sign of apprehension, Ahmad replied, "Thank you, officers, I will be sure to put a thank-you in the credits." Yeah, right, he thought, screw them both. Ahmad was off to his mission to blow up Independence Hall, feeling emboldened.

Chapter 46

Smooth Cone Ice Cream Route
Philadelphia, Pennsylvania

As he turned his specially outfitted 1968 Dodge ice cream truck down Washington Street with the music playing for, who knows, perhaps the fifteen thousandth time, kids came running. This was by far his best street for selling Drumsticks, Popsicles, Fudgsicles, and ice cream sandwiches. He could spend hours taking orders for Drumsticks. It'd been that way since 1972 when Roscoe Grant Coleman began his journey to bring some happiness to a world to which he was forever indebted.

It was January 31, 1968, during the Vietnam War Tet Offensive, Marine Corps Corporal Coleman was fighting for survival as 70,000 Viet Cong and PAVN invaded South Vietnam. In the battle for Hue City, Coleman was fighting alongside his brothers from the 1st Marine Division. As his company of Marines made a tactical withdrawal due to overwhelming numbers of enemy troops, Coleman, along with two other Marines, fired his M-60 machine gun to provide cover fire. Quickly, they found themselves surrounded. As they fought to delay the enemy's advance, all three were shot. With his two comrades dead, Coleman, unconscious from four massive bullet wounds, woke up a short time later in a medical evac helo. As the blades on the Huey thundered, Coleman blinked a few times and passed out again.

Ending up in the 95th Evacuation Hospital and eventually flown stateside, Coleman began the arduous journey to get his life back. Constantly fighting survivor's guilt and grief over the loss of his Marine buddies, Coleman ended up back at his roots in Philadelphia.

Over the years, Coleman never fully recovered but was most at ease seeing the kids running up to his ice cream truck, full of life and without a care in the world. As they stood at the side of his Dodge, deciding what flavorful ice cream to order, he had to smile; it made him so happy, and life seemed more bearable.

"Hi, Mr. Coleman," said a bright-eyed boy named Lucas. Coleman reminisced about how he had served Lucas's grandfather, his father, and now the third generation—all with smiles that could melt your heart.

"What will it be today, Lucas?"

"Well, Mr. Coleman, I have been mowing lawns and have enough saved to buy two Drumsticks, one vanilla and the other the Big Choc."

"Good for you, Lucas, coming right up."

With kids around him like Lucas, life was good. At night, it was another story. Nightmares of all sorts, all dealing with his tour in Vietnam and the battle for Hue. He was now in his 70s; perhaps it was time to retire. But what then, he asked himself.

Philadelphia, Pennsylvania

Ahmad was holed up tight in Philadelphia, preparing for his mission, when he got a secure phone call from an excited Samir Makhlouf. "Ahmad, we have been attacked by the police. Mustafa is dead. I am worried about you and our plan. Praise Allah, should we move forward?"

"Please calm down. Everything happens for a reason with Allah. Everything here is going as we planned. Soon, the infidels from America will pay the price for being non-believers. Allah is with me. I have a strategy that will work and send a message to the world. I will not be in contact with you until the blessed day we blow the Americans from the face of the earth."

Samir said, "Ahmad—" but Ahmad had hung up. Samir prayed for his success. What else could he do? The man was on a mission.

Lucas Residence

Philadelphia, Pennsylvania

Waiting patiently in front of his house as he did each day when he was home, Lucas listened extra hard for his favorite song playing from Mr. Coleman's ice cream truck. The twelve-year-old didn't wear a watch or have a phone but could feel it when it was time for his afternoon treat. After a long wait, he gave up and walked back to his house with his head hung low. Strange, he thought, Mr. Coleman was never late. After telling his mom, who seemed disinterested, he told his neighbor and best friend, Mr. Jackson, who used to be a police officer. Lucas hoped Mr. Jackson would be home soon.

The young boy just knew something must have happened to Mr. Coleman. As Jackson arrived home and got out of his car, Lucas sprinted up to him.

"Mr. Jackson, Mr. Jackson," a breathless Lucas blurted out.

"Woo, slow down, Lucas. What the heck has you so riled up?"

"Mr. Jackson, I didn't get my ice cream today."

"Well, if that's all, I have some cones in my fridge—"

"No, you don't understand, sir," Lucas said, interrupting him mid-sentence, "the ice cream truck never came today.

That's never happened before. I know something must be wrong with Mr. Coleman."

No matter this kid's age, Jackson's instincts told him something was up with Lucas. He decided to make some calls, if nothing else, to calm his little friend down. "Listen, Lucas, I will do some checking and see why Mr. Coleman missed coming by. I'm sure it can be explained. I will let you know as soon as I find something out."

He immediately went into the house and called Brenda, who had handled his precinct for years as a radio operator. She was his last remaining ally in the department.

"Hi, Brenda, it's Jackson. Hey, I have a young boy here who thinks something bad happened to the Smooth Cone ice cream man. Have you heard anything?"

"No, nothing. But I tell you what, this guy must have been punctual, as we received a non-emergency call from some little girl asking about him. You could hear her mom in the background consoling her as she sobbed that the ice cream man never showed up. We can do a safety check on his residence if you think something is happening here."

"You know us cops and our instincts; something tells me this needs a look-into. Please let me know."

"Sure thing, Kordell." An hour later, the security guard from Independence Hall heard that Coleman's home was empty, with no sign of Mr. Coleman or his truck.

Smooth Cone Ice Cream Route

Philadelphia, Pennsylvania

The days around the July 4th holiday were always the best days for selling his ice cream. Roscoe Coleman, as usual, was on his route at precisely 1300 hours. The ex-Marine still used military time because it made so much more sense. His route, like his life, followed a specific course. Given how much business there was, he liked staying on schedule; it was predictable.

As the day progressed, Coleman was driving down a street where he never sold ice cream. This allowed him to shortcut it over to Lincoln Street, which took him on the remainder of his route. As he was mid-block, passing an old cornfield, he saw a man waving his hands at him. Strange, he never had a customer on this street. He slowed down. He thought the man had a friendly smile. Coleman stopped and went to the open window.

"Hello," Coleman said. "How can I help you?"

"Hi," said Ahmad Nadar, "my car broke down a few blocks from here, and I was hoping you could sell me some ice cream and give me a quick lift. I have a bum leg from my time in the Marine Corps, Afghanistan, and can't get around that well."

"Semper fi, brother, hop in. US Marine, Vietnam, 1972."

Coleman opened the back door, even though it was unlocked, to greet the fellow Marine.

Ahmad stepped into the ice cream truck, rapidly pulling out his PC-9 Zoaf with a suppressor, and fired two rounds, one into Coleman's chest and one into his head. Coleman was thrown back inside his truck and hit the floor. A pool of blood quickly formed.

"Praise be to Allah," said the terrorist.

Chapter 47

Independence Day

Hamtramck, Michigan

Jessie Hampton was not one to sit on his hands, especially when his girlfriend, no, now his fiancée of sorts, had been taken hostage by a bunch of Lebanese gangbangers. It was July 4th, and he had a plan to get his girl back.

From what he could deduce from the FBI and the police, these terrorists had plans to take out a power station. The question was which one. Since the group was eyeballing the Rouge Park power-generating plant a few days ago, he reasoned they would not be so stupid as to go back there but would choose another one in the area. He was convinced; find them, and he would find Sarah. Over the past several days, he had used Google Maps and his own recon to locate different stations. He picked the three closest to their original target and planted game cameras at two sites. He would stake out the third site, which seemed the most likely target because of its size. He programmed his phone to receive the camera signal and alert him if they showed up.

He was ready, armed with his Sig Sauer M17. He hit the site at 0230 hours and took cover in a grove of trees.

Chapter 48

Power Generator Station 143

Detroit, Michigan

Sarah understood all too well that her life expectancy was dwindling by the minute. Shoved to the floor of Sabar's jacked-up pickup truck with its twenty-inch knobby tires, she was told if she moved an inch, she would get a bullet in the head. She was becoming a believer. Assholes like these three wannabe terrorists were on a mission, and she was their cover or, she figured, a bargaining chip with the authorities. No matter, she would be dead soon because she could ID all three men. She knew it, they knew it. There was no way she would be kicked loose.

Her time was running out, not unlike when she was flying over the South China Sea in her E-2 Hawkeye during the war with China, with the engine engulfed in flames and burning through the wing of her aircraft. She had quickly devised a plan then and could now—she had to.

"Time check," said Nadar as they bounced along on some nondescript dirt road.

Back came the reply from BM, "3:11," he calmly said, even though he was scared shitless. He still questioned why he had ever been involved with this gang. I guess, he thought, because I'm proud of my Lebanese heritage, and these guys are the only ones who ever treated me like I meant something in this world.

"Listen," said Nadar, "when we get close to the site, we will pull over and take out the two security cameras as we have practiced. You got the Neptune, Aahad?"

"Of course I do," said a fully black-clothed Jabbour.

Pulling up to their pre-arranged position, approximately fifty yards from a camera mounted on a pole above the secure gate, Jabbour jumped from the truck, carrying his military-grade Neptune Blue Burning Laser Pointer. With a clear sight of the camera, Jabbour took aim, zeroed in on the camera lens, and pulled the trigger, instantly disabling it.

Running to his next position, Jabbour repeated his actions and cleared the area for the trio to approach the power station.

As Jessie shifted his weight to his other foot while standing hidden in a grove of trees, he was beginning to second-guess his choice of likely targets. Then he heard the faint sound of a rumbling engine cutting through the still air—then it stopped. He was straining to hear something, anything when he saw streaks of a solid blue laser light directed in the area of the power station. His first instinct was to go for his M17 in its holster on his right hip. Stupid, he thought; he was surely outnumbered. He reminded himself that his most significant strategic advantage was to take these assholes by surprise. If that didn't work, Sarah would be a widow before they were even married—that is if she survived. Moving cautiously and carefully on foot, he started towards the power station.

As the large truck approached the power station, all heads were on a swivel, alert to anything that did not fit the area.

"BM," said his boss, Nadar, "you stay with the girl, monitor the police frequencies, and alert us if any trouble is headed our way. Got it?"

"Yep," came BM's reply.

Leaving the truck running, Nadar and Jabbour grabbed their Browning X-Bolt Hells Canyon bolt-action rifles, quickly jumped from the truck, and headed to the east side of the fenced power station. Both knew exactly what their targets were in the run of power lines and similar-looking nondescript metal boxes.

Contained in each rifle were four blue tip armor-piercing bullets. Both men spread out along the fence; there was no need to gain access inside when they could simply shoot between the openings in the chain link fence. Nadar efficiently aimed at the voltage regulation transformers that send both high and low-voltage electricity for long- and short-term transmission. Nadar aimed and squeezed off his first round. *Boom*. The sharp, piercing crack startled him, but he quickly regained his composure and fired the remaining three rounds, spread out over the transformers. He reloaded as Jabbour fired his rifle, aiming for the site's switching station. Nadar was already adapting to the thunderous blasts that pierced the night silence like a sonic boom. What dim lighting there was quickly extinguished.

Sarah didn't let the crushing sound of gunfire disrupt her plan to escape. When there was a moment of silence, Sarah spoke up. "Bro, you got to let me make a run for it. You know they are going to kill me. You don't want to spend the rest of your life in prison, do you? Now let me out."

BM hesitated, looking scared, "I don't know. If I let you go, they will kill me for sure." His face told the whole story. He was about to say something else when an arm shot through the open door with a gun pointed directly at his head.

"Make one move, asshole, and I will kill you. Now drop your gun."

Sarah couldn't believe her eyes. It was Jessie!

BM hesitated. Sarah yelled, "Do it, BM—now."

He slowly set the gun down on the car seat. Jessie grabbed it. More shots began to ring out.

"Sarah, can you move?"

"Shit yes, what's your plan?"

"We need to get under cover," said Jessie. "Okay, BM, get out of the truck and on your knees."

"No, don't shoot me, please, please don't."

"I'm not going to kill you; now, do as you're told."

As BM got to his knees, Jessie helped Sarah out of the truck, quickly cut the cord cuff, and handed her BM's 9mm.

"Okay," said Jessie, "Take him towards the woods. I will be right behind you."

"Got it," said Sarah. "Come on, BM," she said, pushing him toward the trees. Just then, the shooting stopped. It was eerily quiet. They could hear some talking.

Jessie quickly jumped into the driver's seat of the truck, which was pointing in the direction of the plant, put it in drive, and jumped out. The big truck rolled towards the fence.

Jessie immediately caught up with Sarah and their captive. "Let's go; I have my truck nearby."

FBI Command Post

Grant Elementary School Parking Lot

Sitting together, wearing body armor with the bold letters "FBI" announcing who they were, Harley and Ali were both sipping their second cup of coffee as comms came to life. "All units, we have security cameras offline at Power Generator Station 143. F5 Adam respond."

"Roger that," said Ali calmly, but with his insides shooting adrenaline throughout his body, knowing what this meant.

"Let's go," yelled an unsettled Williamson riding in the back seat.

Harley slammed the car into drive while Ali shouted out preset directions to GS 143.

Twenty thousand feet overhead, a specially outfitted MQ-9 military drone was quickly closing on the area. It was fitted with the latest rendition of the FLIR system, which uses thermal cameras to detect heat differences as small as 0.01C.

As Harley was about to bust through a red traffic light, everything suddenly went dark. As far as the eye could see, nothing but black staring back. The three men looked around and said nothing—they knew.

The radio chatter was increasing. Cutting through commands going out: "Air 10, we have multiple people on the ground at PS 143. We have two running toward a truck at the edge of the plant and three others running in the opposite direction towards another vehicle parked a distance away. All lights in the area and beyond are out."

"We are eleven minutes out," Harley fired back. Monitor the vehicle nearest the plant; that's our guys. Keep us posted."

"Roger that," came the reply.

Power Generator Station 143

Detroit, Michigan

"What the fuck," yelled Umair. His eyes, partially blinded by the muzzle flashes from his rifle, was attempting to adjust to the blackness around him. What he saw was the silhouette of his truck rolling towards the chain link fence surrounding the power station.

"What's going on, Umair?" yelled Aahad.

"How the fuck am I supposed to know," he grunted as the two sprinted over to the truck, rifles at the ready. Looking inside the cab, the leader of the Warren Bros street gang, now turned terrorist, screamed "Shit!" It was empty—no hostage, no BM. He quickly noticed the truck had landed against a support pole to the fence.

"We've got to get moving," blurted Aahad. "The cops will be storming this area in a heartbeat."

"Where the fuck are BM and that bitch?" said Umair. "They couldn't have gone far."

Just then, both men stopped in their tracks as they heard a vehicle start up, and the sound of its strained engine as it roared away. Through the trees, they caught a glimpse of an SUV with its headlights on and tires spinning in the dirt.

"Get in," ordered Umair, "that's our answer."

Putting the truck into 4-wheel drive, Umair attempted to back up, but the metal bar of the fence was caught on the truck's bodywork. Fuck this, he thought. Rocking the truck back and forth, he waited until the weight shifted towards the back and floored it.

The engine screamed, followed by a loud crunching sound as the tires gained traction, busting the truck loose in one giant burst of metal and flying parts as the front bumper was partially torn off. As Umair gunned the engine, the bumper, scraping along the ground, hit a rut, tearing it from the truck. As it flew by, they both unconsciously ducked.

Overhead, the MQ-9 was chronicling everything. "Air 10 to responding units, I have two vehicles eastbound towards

Park Drive. Both are coming from GS 143. It appears that we have some sort of pursuit with both vehicles traveling at a high rate of speed. The vehicle that was closest to the power station is pursuing the other car."

Ali reached for the mike, "F5 Adam, roger."

The SAC spoke first. "What do you guys think?"

Harley answered, "It sounds like we have bad guys chasing good guys. The second vehicle doesn't seem to be with whoever parked next to the power station. But I wonder who that would be?"

"I've got a hunch," said Ali. Who else other than law enforcement would be sniffing around a power station?"

"Shit, you're right, it must be Jessie."

Chapter 49

Park Drive

Detroit, Michigan

Jessie kept glancing in his mirrors. With the entire city blacked out, whatever light there was stood out and the bright lights behind him were closing.

"They are gaining on us," warned Jessie as he maneuvered down Park Drive at 70 mph, as fast as he dared go with traffic lights out and everything pitch black.

Sarah blurted out, "I have an idea." She dialed 911 on Jessie's phone. When it rang, she told Jessie to head to the nearest police station.

"911, what is your emergency? And yes, we are aware of the blackout."

"We are traveling eastbound on Park Drive near Holly Street. Two armed men are chasing us in a raised red Dodge Ram truck. We need assistance quickly."

"Okay," said the calm police dispatcher. "Stay on the line as I put the call out to get a unit rolling. What kind of car are you driving? Sarah told her. She heard the dispatcher putting out the call.

"Great idea, Sarah," said her fiancé.

Tied into the local law enforcement, F5 Adam heard the call. Ali quickly spoke up, “That must be their headlights,” pointing out the front window. Harley made a snap decision and activated the car’s concealed emergency lights, lighting up the night around them with flashing red, blue, and yellow strobes. He stopped the car, aligning it perpendicular to the roadway. All three FBI agents exited the vehicle and grabbed M4 carbines from the trunk.

“What do you make of that,” said Jessie as the bright, flashing lights swallowed up the area around them.

“That was fast,” said Sarah. BM started to push himself up from the floor to sneak a look. “Oh no, you don’t; get your ass back down on the floor before I forget how nice you were.”

“I’m pulling to the side of the road,” exclaimed Jessie. As he pulled to the side of the roadway, he and Sarah saw the barrels of three rifles pointing directly at them. Jessie quickly turned on the dome light, flooding the car's interior with light. They saw Ali and Harley's familiar faces as they carefully approached the vehicle.

Jessie yelled out the window, “Don’t shoot, it’s us, Jessie and Sarah. We have one of the gang members in the back seat. There’s two more right behind us in a truck.”

"Get out and take cover behind our vehicle," yelled Harley. As the three climbed out of the SUV, Ali slapped a pair of handcuffs on BM, who didn't utter a word. As they moved, they saw a pair of headlights slow down and stop in the roadway.

The flashing emergency lights caused the two gang members to slow down and stop as they approached the roadblock. "We must decide this second," said Umair as he looked at his second in command. "Do we run from these infidels, or do we fight?"

"I pray we lead by example," said Aahad, "and commit jihad. The new World awaits us, Alhamdulillah!" With that, both men jumped from the truck and grabbed their high-powered Browning rifles which were each loaded with four blue tip armor-piercing bullets. As they took a position behind their truck, they aimed at the flashing lights and fired. The air around them was filled with a giant *boom* as the rounds raced toward their targets. Quickly, the terrorists squeezed off another round and then another—*boom, boom.*

Seventy yards away, five souls tried to bury themselves even deeper in the dirt shoulder that was sheltering them. As the bullets hit, the sound of crunching metal gave off an eerie sound of impending death. The three agents immediately returned fire, spraying rounds at the large truck with its lights still on. As the terrorists' second shots came in, one round traveled through the SUV as if it were made of balsa wood, striking BM squarely in the head, splattering parts of his skull in a ten-foot bloody radius. All three agents, peering through the blood on their faces, emptied their magazines, firing back toward the muzzle flashes.

"Fuck this," screamed Harley over the din of fire. "I'm going to flank those pricks. Cover me." Without waiting for an answer, the former Marine crouched down and ran twenty yards into a field near the large truck as Jessie joined the other two agents in laying down cover fire.

On the receiving end of the barrage of bullets, both terrorists wiggled behind the giant tires of their truck. Suddenly, a round ricocheted off the pavement, striking Aahad in his lower leg. He yelled out in pain, "I'm hit." Blood immediately began gushing out from the large wound. Pushing back against the pain, he reloaded.

As Aahad was getting ready to fire again, Harley got into a position where he could make out the silhouettes of the two men. An expert shot in the Marines as well as with the FBI, he let loose with a magazine of controlled fire, marching his rounds across the roadway until they found their mark on the unsuspecting men. Both were hit almost simultaneously, the impacts bouncing them around like rag dolls. Harley saw one of the men move and fired two more rounds into his upper body. Everything went still. "Hold your fire," he yelled, "suspects down."

Out of the corner of his eye, he saw help arriving from behind the FBI vehicle. Harley, with his rifle outstretched, cautiously moved towards the two prone men. There was no movement, and blood was everywhere. As he neared the gang members, the two other FBI agents joined him, and all three examined the suspects for any sign of life. There was none. Harley directed Ali to handcuff the two dead men as he had been trained to do. No one said a word. They all were thankful to be alive.

Chapter 50

Philadelphia, Pennsylvania

The news was sobering as the nation awoke to a July 4th holiday. The media reported an attack at a power distribution center in Dearborn, Michigan, that knocked out electricity to several surrounding states. Authorities were tight-lipped about the attack, commenting that it was an ongoing investigation.

While the agencies remained secretive, social media didn't miss a beat as footage beamed from phone to internet showed two dead bodies behind a pickup truck near the power plant. It was a bloody mess, and citizens asked what was happening. Despite being an enormous story, it was offset by people's indifference to a constant bombardment of violence blasting from their phones and TVs. It was much more straightforward to turn that nonsense off and instead move ahead with planning their Independence Day celebrations—where they would go for the real fireworks. So what if the lights were out, it would make the fireworks that night more spectacular.

In Philadelphia, the celebrations had begun weeks before the big day. Kicking it off was the Wawa Welcome America celebration commemorating Juneteenth. There were concerts featuring Demi Lovato and Ludacris. All this culminated with a breathtaking celebration of America's independence with a massive fireworks show.

At 10:00 a.m., the mayor and several notable guest speakers comfortable on the raised portable stage were about to welcome the hundreds of spectators packing the grass parkway in front of the iconic Independence Hall. It was a perfect day as the mayor prepared for his favorite event of the year and his reading of the Declaration of Independence.

Also preparing for the celebration, but for different reasons, was a phalanx of FBI, Philadelphia PD, and state police—many in plainclothes. With a credible threat in play, every precaution was being taken. Overhead, police helicopters circled the venue, making their presence known. Above them, but much more discreet, was a military MQ-9 Reaper. There was also the battery of Avenger Air Defense Systems atop a 17-story building located near Independence Hall.

On the ground, Kordell Jackson was acting on a hunch. It was something he felt in his gut. Call it whatever you want, but for street cops like Kordell, you never make excuses for these instincts molded from years of combating criminals—or terrorists, for that matter. You have an instinct, and you act on it—period.

His boss at Independence Hall didn't like him roaming around; he told him that his place was at the Hall, not out on the streets. But when Kordell pleaded his case—that there were so many law enforcement officers bumping into one another in and around the Hall that he wasn't needed—he finally convinced his superior to turn him loose. So here he was, dressed in plain clothes, hanging out on Arch Street with a clear two-block view of Independence Hall. He could feel his Glock 19 pressing against his side. A comforting awareness.

Chapter 51

Philadelphia, Pennsylvania

Ahmad Nadar woke up rested and energized from his night's sleep, knowing this was the day the infidels of the US would remember for all eternity. As the sun peeked through his drawn curtains, Ahmad faced Mecca for his Fajr prayer. He was at peace but wanted to seek Allah's blessings and guidance before he set out to complete his task of blowing up Independence Hall. It was July 4th, and the US was about to pay a huge price for being non-believers.

As he prepared for what was most likely his last day on Earth, he had Alexa play his news brief. He was delighted to hear of a four-state blackout from his brother-in-arms of the destruction of a relay station in Dearborn. He was somewhat saddened to hear of their deaths but knew he would soon join them in the afterlife as a fellow martyr. Ahmad understood this was just the distraction needed to divert attention from Independence Hall.

Walking to his oversized garage, his thoughts were now directed to his mission. As his training instructors had taught him, preparation for a mission is one of the keys to success. As he entered the garage, the first thing he saw was the dead ice cream driver he had propped against the garage wall, staring back at him with a bullet hole neatly placed in his forehead. Sorry buddy, but this is war, he reflected.

The ice cream route truck was ready. It had a full gas tank, and the side access panel where kids order treats was open and tucked into place. It would have a specific purpose today, and it wasn't serving ice cream. He stepped into the old truck, which had blood splattered around the interior. None of that mattered now; he was getting ready to head out.

Lying neatly on the floor were the two M72 rocket launchers loaded with anti-structure munitions. Ahmad prepared the single-shot launchers for firing. He removed the pull pin, the front cover, and the adjustable sling. Next, he grasped the launcher and sharply pulled his hands in opposite directions, causing the weapon to fully extend into the firing position. He then reversed his actions and tried to force the launcher closed. It didn't budge, which told him it was locked in place and ready to fire. Ensuring the ice cream theme music was turned off, he started the engine and headed toward his destiny.

Lucas woke up early. It was July 4th, and that meant fireworks. He loved the noise, the smoke, and the beauty of the explosions with so many different glittering lights. Besides Christmas, this was the best day of the year for him.

The twelve-year-old was brushing his teeth as he studied himself in the mirror. Staring back at him were his big hazel eyes, neatly trimmed blond hair, and, if a toothbrush were not stuck in his mouth, his cute perpetual smile. Yes, this was going to be a great day.

But there was a downside, he considered, and that was going to Independence Hall early to hear the mayor read the Declaration of Independence, something he did every 4th. Boring. Oh well, they at least play some great patriotic music. He also hoped to see his friend and neighbor, Mr. Jackson, who worked security there. He thought Mr. Jackson was the coolest guy because he treated him nicely. Once, he even let Lucas go on patrol around the Hall, where he couldn't stop staring at the big gun Mr. Jackson carried on his hip. All of this made him miss his dad even more. His pop died two years ago in a traffic accident. Boy, how he missed him.

Interrupting his thoughts, he heard his mom yell, "C'mon Lucas, we don't want to be late."

"Okay, Mom, here I come." Five minutes later, they were on the way to Independence Hall.

As Kordell walked the grassy parkway, he was convinced if Nadar was dumb enough to try and commit an act of terrorism against Independence Hall, it wouldn't be up close and personal. No, it would come from a safe distance away. Perhaps a rooftop nearby—or on foot, he didn't know—but Arch Street provided the most extended, uninterrupted view of the Hall. He was headed that way.

Riding towards the Hall with his mom, Lucas was daydreaming as he looked out the window. He loved riding shotgun in the front, still recalling those days of sitting in the back seat in his booster. No, he reflected, I'm a big boy now.

Knocking him out of his daze was the sight of Mr. Coleman's ice cream truck as it filled his view out the side window. "Mom, there's the ice cream truck. Pull alongside so I can wave." As she pulled even with the truck from the left lane, both looked at the driver. Lucas began to wave but stopped immediately, his hand frozen in air. This wasn't his friend, but someone else. Why would he be driving the ice cream truck?

"Mom, that's not Mr. Coleman, something must be wrong. Mr. Coleman is the only man I ever saw driving the ice cream truck." Just then, the man turned his head, staring right through the twelve-year-old, scaring him to death. His mom slammed on the brakes, disturbed by what they had just seen. The man had a look of evil that she would never forget.

"Mom, we must do something. That wasn't Mr. Coleman."

Thinking quickly, Lucas's mom pulled over and took out her cell phone. She knew Kordell, her neighbor, was working today, and he would know what to do.

"Hello, what's up, Helen? I'm at work right now."

"I know, that's why I'm calling. Lucas and I just saw Mr. Coleman's ice cream truck with some weird guy driving. He glared at us and terrified us both. Lucas is worried sick."

"Okay," said Kordell, "where did you last see him? Be specific."

"Let me see. Yeah, we were heading east on Race Street near North Broad."

"And you are both sure this is the right ice cream truck?"

"Of course," Helen answered, "my son has grown up getting ice cream from Mr. Coleman and that truck for years. No, something is wrong."

"Did the man appear to be Middle Eastern?"

She hesitated a second, "Yes, he did."

Kordell hurriedly ended the call, "Thanks, Helen. I will take it from here. Goodbye."

Kordell wasted no time; he didn't like what he had just heard. It had to be Nadar, he thought. He quickly pulled out his APX radio from his back pocket. "Control, FB-1, a witness states she just saw our suspect, Ahmad Nadar, driving a possible stolen ice cream truck east on Race Street near North Broad. Additionally, the owner of the vehicle is reported missing."

As the RTO repeated his call, Kordell walked past the Visitor Center. He quickly moved north toward Arch Street, bordering the National Constitution Center. As he cut across the open grassy park, it took a moment to get eyes on Arch Steet just east of 6th because of the landscape. As he cleared some trees, he saw it. Parked on the wrong side of Arch was an ice cream truck, with the side of the vehicle facing Independence Hall wide open. Kordell immediately noticed there was no music blaring from its prominent white speaker and no kids. Suddenly, he saw the tip of a metal object extending out of the truck, aimed in the direction of Independence Hall. Shit, he thought, that has to be some shoulder-fired munitions. He was fifty yards away, now sprinting as fast as he could toward the truck.

Chapter 52

Arch Street near 6th Street

Philadelphia, Pennsylvania

As Ahmad Nadar cruised toward his destiny, driving the ice cream truck, he was relaxed and focused. In fact, he couldn't believe how calm he was as he drove east on Race Street. Everything was going exactly as he had planned. He took a minute to reflect on his Hezbollah terrorist training and Allah for putting him in this Zen state of mind. He visualized his target and saw two rockets roaring toward Independence Hall, leaving a smoke trail behind.

Interrupting his vision was some dumbass kid waving at him from a car traveling next to him. He first saw him out of the corner of his eye, but as he looked over, the kid stopped waving with a look of recognition that Ahmad was not who the kid expected to see driving this ice cream truck. He saw the woman driver get the same look of fear, and he checked his mirrors as she slammed on her brakes and pulled to the side of the road. As he continued, she appeared to be talking on her cell phone. He didn't like any of this, but he was only blocks away from his launching point on Arch Street. No one could stop him now.

As he pulled up on Arch Street, he turned left against a one-way street, crossing over through the opposing traffic lane with the right side of the truck facing towards Independence Hall. With the side panel already open, he slammed the truck into park and hurriedly took a position in the back. He reached down, grabbed the first M72, and raised it, using the counter as a sort of tripod for his arms to steady his aim. There were eighteen windows neatly spaced on the two-story building. He took aim at the bottom floor window, fourth from the right.

Ahmad was in tune with his body's respiratory pause thanks to his training. As he finished exhaling naturally, not forcing the air out, he took his next breath slowly and cut it off halfway through his breathing cycle. He couldn't believe how relaxed he was. His finger slid to the trigger bar, and he gently pushed it, which caused the firing pin to strike the primer, igniting the black powder in the flash tube and exploding the propellant in the rocket motor.

A powerful, sharp whoosh sound echoed off the nearby buildings as the rocket left the launcher. People stopped what they were doing. Heads turned toward the source of the sound. The mayor stopped mid-sentence in his recital of the Declaration of Independence. He looked up and saw black smoke in the air, followed by a massive explosion. It would be the last thing the mayor of Philadelphia would ever see as a chunk of the building shot through the air, hitting him in the side of the head and killing him instantly. Immediately, people in the area were screaming and running to escape whatever was happening.

The concussion from the anti-structure munition hit its target perfectly, blowing out the glass and brick in a 360-degree radius, killing scores of people inside and around the building. Seconds later, the survivors heard another loud whoosh.

Kordell was focused on the truck as he sprinted in that direction, using every ounce of power his legs could deliver. Abruptly, he saw a smoke-filled flash and heard a loud whooshing sound. He felt the pressure from the blast push his skin against his body. He stumbled and fell into a somersault, his momentum returning him upright. He pulled out his Glock and looked for a target, but he could only see a smoke-filled area around the truck. Another bright blast ripped through the air as he tried to locate the suspect. This time, he dove to the ground, lying prone, constantly scanning the area. He could feel the second explosion shake the ground. He heard screams and saw people running in every direction. It was complete chaos, but he forced himself to stay focused.

Chapter 53

Independence Hall
Philadelphia, Pennsylvania

The second warhead found its mark, crashing through window three on the upper floor, exploding as it bore through the inner wall. A tour group of twenty was just entering the room, including a young married couple from Ohio taking their first vacation with their 10-month-old little girl. They all were instantly vaporized from the massive detonation. Later, a picture of the three went viral. It had been taken by a press photographer, who snapped the photo because he thought they looked like the perfect July 4th family. They were all dressed in similar colorful patriotic outfits with the picturesque Independence Hall in the background. The proud parents wore bright smiles, and even their baby had a grin. The image came to represent the innocence of the victims who had simply been going about their lives celebrating their country's Independence Day.

For most, the most recognizable part of the Hall is its 168-foot-tall bell tower and steeple, constructed in 1828. As the fires ripped through the historic symbol of American democracy, the building was engulfed in flames. Survivors and first responders couldn't help but look up as the bell tower retained its shape even as it came crashing down in a ball of fire, adding to the already burning inferno.

Philadelphia Fire Department Engine 8, Ladder 2, and Medics 44 and 63B led the response to Independence Hall. In the short time after the first warhead struck, units were rolling. Pulling up in his specially equipped SUV was Battalion Chief 4, Jacob Devries, who took one look at the carnage surrounding his beloved Independence Hall and yelled over his comms, "This is an all hands sit; Independence Hall is completely engulfed. I want every ambulance in the city to respond and every hospital to prepare for hundreds of injured."

As he began directing equipment and firefighters into position, he felt someone grab his back. What the hell, he thought. He would never forget what he saw when he turned around. It was a woman in her 30s, with her blond hair still smoldering and facial burns so severe she didn't even look human. She kept screaming, "Where's Susie? Where's my little girl?" over and over. At that moment, two paramedics rushed over to assist, allowing the chief to return to the responding units, which were now coming in from all over the city. As he gently handed the young woman over and walked away, he could continue to hear her scream. Then he noticed she was not the only one in agony. All over the grounds were scores of people either dead or screaming for help. "Help me, please help me," echoed from face to face. He scolded himself to get control and return to what he needed to do: deploy his firefighters.

Arch Street – Between S. 6th and S. 5th Street

Philadelphia, Pennsylvania

Kordell jumped up from the ground, and as he ran towards the ice cream truck, he saw flames start to leap out of the open side. Suddenly, a man jumped from the truck, sprinting down Arch Street towards South 5th. As the man ran, he glanced over his shoulder, and Kordell recognized him. It was Nadar. He ran faster.

An older woman in a 2015 Toyota Camry was stopped in the left lane on Arch. She had her driver's window down, enjoying the fresh air of the July morning. Sitting at the red light, she looked a half block ahead and saw what looked like an ice cream truck on fire. She decided she would have to get over a lane to avoid it. The woman failed to notice a man running down the street in her direction as she checked her mirrors, but when she looked back, she saw him for the first time, running up to her car with a gun in his hand. Before she could even scream, Nadar shot her in the head and quickly opened her door, throwing her dead body into the street like discarded trash.

Kordell saw it all. He was approaching the intersection when Nadar floored the gas pedal and took off, squealing the tires. Kordell stepped partially into the roadway to get a better shot, leveling his Glock 19 at Nadar. He pounded round after round into the car's windshield, shattering it. Nadar was now coming right at him; Kordell kept firing, finally seeing an explosion of blood fill the air around Nadar's head. As the terrorist sped by him, the car struck Kordell on his left side, spinning him around like a top and landing him entirely down in the roadway. He heard a massive crash as the car smashed straight into the burning ice cream truck. Managing to look up, he saw the Toyota crumpled against the front of the Dodge truck. An enormous fiery explosion followed, throwing burning debris high into the air, with some of it landing around him.

Kordell glanced down at his leg and saw it was facing in a direction it had no right to. There was blood—his blood—everywhere. The pain was unbearable. He heard voices and felt himself being dragged away from the hot, burning wreckage by a passerby. Then there was nothing.

Chapter 54

Hamtramck, Michigan

As the morning sun snuck through the partially open blind, it settled on Sarah's slumbering face. She unconsciously incorporated it into her dream as a bright flash of Independence Hall burning to the ground. That woke her up. As she wiped the thought from her mind, she smelled fresh coffee. That's more like it, she thought. Then it hit her. Shit, this is my wedding day. She jumped out of bed like some jock, landed in her slippers, and was off to the kitchen, where her husband-to-be was hanging out by the coffee maker. Jessie could barely respond as Sarah jumped through the air right into his quickly opening arms. Sarah gave him a long, passionate kiss. "Oh, Jessie, I'm so excited. This is our day, baby." With that, she kissed him again, making this one count for more.

"No shit!" was all Jessie could get out at first. "Wow, what an entry, sweetheart."

"Oh, Jessie, I'm just so happy we've made this decision. I love you so much." That comment was followed by kiss three.

"Whoa, girl, much more of that, and we won't make it to the JP in time." He kissed her back just as his future father-in-law came into the room.

"Okay, kids, calm down or get a room."

Seeing her dad's big smile, Sarah went to him and gave him a huge hug, catching him off guard. He hugged her back. Deep down, he could tell that whatever was trying to kill him had decided to give up, and he was feeling so much better. He was ecstatic to be alive to witness this moment, this day. Sarah was a handful, but oh my gosh, how he loved her.

"Good morning, sir," said Jessie.

"I wish you would just call me Duke, like everyone else."

"Yes, sir. I mean, yes, sir, Duke. Shit, I mean Duke."

"That's better. Now that you will be part of the family, we can be buds."

"Roger that…Duke."

It had been a week since the terrorist attack on Independence Hall. Although Sarah's face still showed signs of the beating she received while in captivity, her spirit was undamaged, and she—like the rest of the nation—wanted payback. Sarah was so happy for her dad since her father was coming around—with the doctors still unable to say why or what from. He didn't deserve what he had been through; no one did. She had told him she would return to the *Reagan* next week. He said he was happy for her and would be fine. He mentioned he was thinking about becoming active again in his local Porsche club, which he loved not only for the cars but mainly for the great people.

Amid all the excitement, Jessie received an emergency call saying his leave had been revoked and that he had to report back to the USS *Ford* immediately. Things were brewing. He would leave tomorrow.

Chapter 55

Situation Room

White House, West Wing, Washington, DC

As President Taylor entered the Situation Room, he first noticed that the 5,000-square-foot room was as packed as he had ever seen it. He was glad he had a reserved seat. It had been a week since the unthinkable happened: the destruction of Independence Hall. Added to that were the 108 souls lost and hundreds wounded. It seemed like a bad dream that you would be so happy to wake up from to most Americans. But that would not happen today and not for the next week—not ever.

Across the world, eight billion people believed their lives might depend on the decisions made in this room. Those in the Middle East were already busy digging shelters against the onslaught they knew was coming. Today, the choices made would go a long way toward answering those questions, which would alter history forever.

Elena Ramirez, the DNI was seated directly across from the president, had been with him since he first became involved with political office so many years ago in Pennsylvania—yes, that Pennsylvania. Hell, his first run for office was announced on the steps of Independence Hall. In these ensuing years, she had never seen the person she believed in so strongly as distressed and determined to solve the complex issues surrounding the Islamic Republic of Iran. No, not even during the war with China five years ago was he this upset. The hammer was going to fall; the question was how hard. Today would determine that impact.

As he walked to his seat, the president said, "Seats, please." There was a noise of shuffling chairs as the assembled group all sat—all but one, that is.

Office of the Supreme Leader

Tehran, Islamic Republic of Iran

President Taylor was not the only person holding a history-altering meeting. So was the Supreme Leader of Iran, Amir Massad. Eight and a half hours ahead of the infidels of Washington, Massad had gathered his ruling elite, who all knew they were there, to provide a body so as to nod their heads yes to Massad's command and proposals. It wasn't hard to do; those still present had been doing it for some time, including the nod of approval earlier for the destruction of Independence Hall.

Also in attendance was Samir Makhlouf, who had slipped out of the US after coordinating the attack against the Americans. Now, he would learn that more essential duties awaited him. Every man in the room knew something else was brewing, something much more ominous against the Americans.

Roxborough Memorial Hospital

Philadelphia, Pennsylvania

Sitting with his former wife by his bedside, Kordell Jackson was happy to be alive after being run over during Nadar's escape attempt. Thank heavens, it was Nadar who was dead. He was dinged up pretty bad, but there was nothing that would stop him from fully recovering.

One of the first visitors he could remember was Lucas, who cried when he first saw Kordell with tubes in his arm and bandages all over his body. Kordell managed to hug the youngster with his one good arm and told him everything was going to be okay. When Kordell told the young boy what he did was so important in stopping the terrorist from getting away, Lucas had an immense smile on his face. He was so proud of himself.

As Kordell was quickly becoming a national hero, his former wife and his two girls were there for him. They stayed in shifts, with at least one family member always present. He and Alice had some long talks about the future. She could tell, as could the girls, that the demons that took over his life after his partner's death were now just becoming a sad, distant memory, with the prospects of their lives together again being genuine.

Even the chief of police came by and asked him if he was ready to return to the job. There would be plenty of mental and physical tests, but the Philadelphia PD wanted him back. Kordell wanted nothing more than to pin that shield he loved so much back on his chest. He felt ready.

Justice of the Peace

Detroit, Michigan

They were all there in the small room used for just such an occasion, called the Marry Room by many. Sarah and Jessie were smartly dressed in their navy dress whites, adorned by rows of shining medals. Sarah wore long pants, refusing to be seen in a Navy skirt, which wasn't her style. Her dad didn't have a uniform, so he wore his Vietnam veteran's hat. They asked their new friends from the FBI, Agents Jennings, and Mohsen, to be their witnesses.

As they entered the Marry Room, both agents were already waiting. Sarah and Jessie did a double take as they entered. Harley was wearing his Marine Corps dress uniform. Even though he was retired, he was still in the Reserves and looked like he could still kick ass. Standing next to him was Ali, dressed in traditional Lebanese formal attire. He wore a tunic art silk kurta pajama and scarf and looked fabulous. Sarah thought what great guys they were to take time out of their lives to attend this wedding. It meant so much after what all of them had been through. Spontaneously, they all had a group hug.

The JP came in and started the service. As Sarah looked deep into Jessie's eyes, she didn't know what the future would bring, but by God, they would do it together, as husband and wife.

Epilogue

Carrier Strike Group 5 - USS *Ronald Reagan*
Arabian Sea

It had been nearly three months since Lieutenant Commander Sarah "Danger" Freeman had sat in the left seat of the Northrop Grumman E-2D Hawkeye. Sitting here reminded her just how much she missed it. Cruising over the Arabian Sea at 25,000 feet, she was rejoining the crew of the *Reagan* as all hell was about to break loose in this part of the world. She was thankful she would be part of the delivery team.

Only weeks after enduring the trauma of being taken hostage, her face still bore lingering traces of the violence inflicted upon her. Most of which she hid under her makeup.

Checking her aircraft instruments for the umptieth time, satisfied, she let her mind drift. Her first thought was how much she missed Jessie. Married for less than two weeks, they were apart again, not only apart but with the strong possibility of a war with Iran and who knows what else. But they both had peace of mind knowing they would soon rotate stateside where they could pick up where they left off. Until then, they both will do their thing, he flying an F-35 off the

Ford and her the Hawkeye off the *Reagan.* Hell, they may even be neighbors of sorts as she heard rumors of a Task Force forming up that would include both their aircraft carriers plus the *Nimitz*. She, along with the world, was waiting for how the US would respond to the terrorist attack on Independence Hall. It sure appeared that they would position themselves as part of the spearhead. That was fine for both of them; this is what they do, and they lived for it.

"Ma'am, twenty miles out," said her copilot, Robert Winston.

"Roger that, I have the controls."

"Yes, ma'am, you have the controls."

As she banked into her approach to the *Reagan*, she heard Winston call out, "85 percent throttle." Sarah hit the second wire perfectly. Her mind was clear, and she was ready to play quarterback from her Hawkeye for what she knew was coming—War.

Red Lines, the sequel to *Attack from Within*, will be released in 2025 as part of the *Sea of Red* three-book series. The story continues.

James Bultema

www.ingramcontent.com/pod-product-compliance
Lightning Source LLC
Chambersburg PA
CBHW030359310726
48979CB00001B/365

* 9 7 9 8 9 8 8 0 7 5 1 3 4 *